Lalla Kezich was born in Trieste and lives today in Rome. In 1977 she published her first collection of stories, *Marina Indiana*. In 1982 she won a major Italian literary award, the "Premio Aquileia", with her novel *La Preparazione*, while this new collection of stories won the "Premio Basilicata" 1985, and was short-listed for the prestigious "Premio Ascona" in Switzerland. She has also worked a good deal in the theatre along with her husband, the noted film critic and playwright Tullio Kezich.

GW00708182

Composition with

translated by John Gatt

dark centre

short stories by Lalla Kezich

Olive Press

First published in Great Britain in 1986
by The Olive Press (Co-operative),
Flat 2, 92 Great Titchfield Street, London WIP 7AG
Originally published as *Gruppo Concentrico*
by Camunia editrice srl, Brescia, 1985

Translation © John Gatt 1986
Original © Lalla Kezich 1985

Cover painting by Felix Vallotton, 1899
© private collection, Zurich

Photoset by Rapidset and Design Ltd, London WC1
Printed in Great Britain by WBC Print Limited,
Barton Manor, St Philips, Bristol

ISBN 0 946889 09 0 pbk
ISBN 0 946889 10 4 hbk

Trade Distribution: *Britain and Ireland*
South of England, the South West and South Wales:
Turnaround Distribution, 27 Horsell Road, London N5 (01-609 7836)
The rest of Britain and Ireland: Scottish and Northern
Book Distribution, 18 Granby Row, Manchester (061-228
3903) and 48A Hamilton Place, Edinburgh (031-225 4950)
United States Bookpeople, 2929 Fifth Street, Berkeley, CA 94710.
(415) 549 3030
Inland Book Company, 22 Hemingway Avenue, East Haven,
CT 06512. (203) 467 4257
Australia Allbooks Distribution, 16 Darghan Street, Glebe, NSW 2037.
(02) 692 0166
Netherlands E. R. Ruward, Spui 231, 2511 BP Den Haag. (070) 636879

Contents

Ida and the signora

Ida looked at the signora, widening her dark eyes, and said: "Think of it, signora. Think of it. My mother's arriving tomorrow." She was silent for a moment, smiled and added: "It's true, isn't it? – you've only got one mother."

The signora took a hurried breath and said: "Yes, yes."

Ida pulled back the headscarf which she'd bound over her head to keep the dust off and said: "I'm very attached to my family. If you only knew how attached I am. When I got to Rome for the first time I cried quite a bit. Can you imagine, a child of fourteen?"

The signora smiled briefly and replied: "Come along. Now you're almost eighteen. One isn't really a child at your age."

"I feel I'm a child," said Ida, and she looked at the signora. "I really do feel a child." She took a few listless steps forward as far as the middle of the room and said: "Well, tell me the truth – a mother, parents anyway, shouldn't send their daughter away at fourteen. What do you say, signora? What do you say?"

The signora seemed to be reflecting, then replied unhappily: "Maybe they needed you to work. You mustn't judge your parents."

Ida pressed her fingers into her neck, making red patches appear on her skin.

"No, no. If they really didn't want me to leave, they wouldn't have sent me away. They'd have found some other way of getting by."

The signora had finished combing her hair, she looked at herself in the mirror, tapped her fingers across her forehead and said: "I have to go out now."

Ida ran to fetch her cape and helped the signora on with it, searched, in some agitation, for her glasses and handbag, and handed them to her. Her face was clouded and her eyes red. The signora gave her a sidelong glance and thought: she's emotionally unstable. God, how unstable she is.

"My mother will be pleased to meet you. My sister, too." Ida opened the lift door, let the signora past and went on: "I'm glad you're meeting my mother, too. Poor woman, you know, I'm sorry for her."

The signora stepped towards the door and asked: "Is this it? Shall I ring?"

The door opened gently and Ida's mother appeared in the narrow opening.

"How like you she is," the signora said at once, and she held out her hand to the woman. The woman's married daughter came up behind her, carrying a baby.

"Do come in," she said, "make yourself at home."

They went into the parlour, which was crammed with heavy rustic furniture that almost reached the ceiling and a rectangular table with chairs ranged all askew around it.

"Please, do make yourself at home," repeated the married daughter, "while I make some coffee."

"Coo, coo, coo," went Ida, reaching out to pick up the infant. "Do you see what a lovely little nephew I've got?"

The signora smiled and turned to Ida's mother: "Are you pleased?" she asked. "Are you pleased with your grandson?"

The woman smiled. She had a longish face, thin lips momentarily curving upwards. She glanced at the lace centre-piece on the table, smoothed out an edge, and replied: "You can imagine: my first grandchild, a boy."

There was a moment's silence. Ida uttered a little cry and said: "Oh, God. He's wet me all over."

She jumped to her feet and informed her sister: "Rosa, I'm putting the baby in his cot."

"Are you staying long?" the signora asked Ida's mother. "Did you have a good journey?"

The woman sighed and said: "The sea was rough. Especially at daybreak, and I was a bit – pardon me – sea-sick."

Rosa came in with the coffee-tray and espresso-cups. She laid everything out on the table and started pouring. She was smaller than Ida, her eyes and her bearing looked reserved and restless.

The signora glanced about her and remarked: "You do have a nice house. You've got all you need."

"Yes, yes," said Rosa, "I can't complain. Though it is small and we do live so far away."

Ida reappeared without the child, sat down at the table and took her cup. Her mother heaved a sigh, gestured at Ida and enquired in a low voice: "Is she any good? Tell me. Tell me the truth."

The signora gave an embarrassed smile and nodded. The mother heaved another sigh and asked: "Does she obey? Does she do everything she ought?"

"Yes, of course," Ida butted in. "I do, I do. Don't you worry."

The woman creased her brow and resumed: "She's alert, you know, signora. She can be very good when she wants to. But sometimes when she was with us she used to make me angry. More than any of the others."

The signora shook her head and repeated: "No, no, she is doing well. We're pleased with her. Well, there's one thing I might say." She reflected for a moment as to whether she should mention it, looked the woman in the eye and went on. "Well, it's that I do find her emotional for her age."

Ida's mother raised her eyes towards the ceiling and replied: "Yes, yes, that's true. But you mustn't mind her. That's just the way she is."

"How do you mean, the way I am?" Ida intervened, her eyes alive and wide awake. "What is the way I am? You're my mother, you ought to know, oughtn't you? You know me better than anyone else, don't you?" Her voice became louder and she began talking rapidly in Sardinian.

Her mother looked away and muttered: "Drop that."

Ida turned to the signora and said: "Do forgive me, I nearly always speak Sardinian at home, it comes more naturally. But I didn't say anything, I said I was wicked, that she's got a wicked daughter."

She broke into laughter. She looked at her mother and laughed, slightly red-faced, and her slender shoulders were quivering. She put her hands over her face and every now and then gasped through her laughter: "Oh, God! Oh, God!"

3

Her mother watched her in silence, pursed her lips, and an offended look darkened her face.

"Stupid girl," she whispered under her breath, "stupid girl."

The baby could be heard wailing from the next room. The women all pricked up their ears. Rosa stood up and said: "He doesn't like being wet. I'll have to get him changed."

Ida had stopped laughing. She looked uneasy, and said: "It is nice here, isn't it?" She also rose to her feet, gathered the coffee cups back on to the tray, and went on: "I think it's time we went. If the dottore gets back, he won't find dinner ready." She looked at her mother and murmured: "I'll come round on Sunday. Goodbye."

They gathered again at the front door, Rose carrying her baby and her mother with hands joined in front and her face long and expressionless. She rested her hand lightly on the signora's arm, and went back to the subject of Ida: "After all, she's young," she said in a dead voice. "Show her some sympathy. Be a mother to her."

On the bus, Ida struggled for a seat and said: "Here, signora, here."

So they sat next to one another, silent. When the bus headed in towards the city from the outskirts, lights and chaos whirled around them. The signora lifted her hand to her forehead.

"Are you feeling bad?" Ida asked at once. "Is your head aching?"

"No," answered the signora, "it's just that I'm a little tired." And she felt a weight around her heart that went on oppressing her for some days.

Ida set the fruit bowl in the middle of the table, contemplated it and remarked: "It's beautiful, isn't it?"

The signora nodded. Ida went round the table and mum-

4

bled: "Everything's here, everything." Then she said: "I do like persimmons. Very much. I always have, ever since I was little."

She recalled something that had happened when she was first in service. Her signora had bought a basket of persimmons and placed them on top of the refrigerator. She was dying to have one, but was too shy to ask and hadn't yet understood whether or not she could help herself to something she felt like having. Unable to hold out, she'd picked up one of the fruits and rushed into her room to munch it away as fast as she could. The fruit oozed a little and set her teeth on edge, it wasn't quite ripe. So, standing there beside the laundry-basket, she burst into tears. She was munching and sobbing and she'd sobbed again later, during the night, in retrospect. And she kept wondering: If I told the signora, what would she say? For at that instant I felt so strange, less than a nothing, and I just couldn't hold back my tears.

She blushed violently, the signora noticed and asked: "What's wrong? Aren't you well?"

Ida touched her middle and answered: "No, I've had a pain here all night long."

"Have a rest," said the signora, "and take something for it."

Ida shook her head: "No, no," she said, "I'm too busy."

The signora's face darkened and she snapped back: "It can wait till tomorrow. If you're not well, you're not to work."

"But I'm not feeling that bad. I assure you, it's getting better."

"Ida, your nerves are bad. I'm sure you think you're ill, but it's only your nerves."

Ida replied: "What can I do about it? Yes, I am nervy, but not quite as much as you think. And anyway, I've always been that way. I get very little sleep, you know. I sleep three or four hours a night."

The signora sat down, looked at this slip of a girl, at her pale, narrow face, at her eyes, beautiful, intelligent – yes, she thought – intelligent eyes, she gave her a smile and said: "Ida, you must cheer yourself up. Just think: you're eighteen, you're nice, and pretty, too. You have so much to be happy about."

"No," said Ida, "no. I can't keep in mind all these things

5

you're mentioning. My mind's on quite different things. My mind's on my sister Giulia, and on my parents who are getting old and can't survive unless I send money home. And I keep thinking about clothes, too."

"Clothes?"

Ida suddenly carried out a graceful movement: she drew herself up a little, with her hands touching her sides. She repeated: "Yes, clothes. Don't you like them, signora? I love them, and I'd like to have thousands." She laughed silently to herself: her eyes lit up and she stood gazing at imaginary shop-fronts arrayed with dresses, skirts, blouses and all the other extraordinary things the city had to offer.

Ida shouted into the telephone. She was speaking Sardinian and the signora came to the door and said: "Don't shout. I don't like shouting."

Ida lowered her voice and carried on speaking rapidly. Her words sounded totally foreign to the signora's ear, even funny, and made her want to laugh. She went into the sitting-room, which had already been tidied up. The sun fell on the pictures, the prints, the Persian rugs, and everything wore a gracious and a smiling air. The signora laid her fingers on the side of a vase, closed a drawer, looked around and picked up the newspaper.

Ida replaced the receiver, took up her broom again, gathered up the sweepings. She went into the kitchen, opened and re-covered the dustbin. She performed a few mechanical movements, then went into the sitting-room. She looked at the signora but said nothing.

"What is it?" enquired the signora, who could sense that she was standing close by, hanging her head. "What is it?"

"Nothing," answered Ida with a sigh. "Nothing."

"Is everything laid in? Have you ordered the groceries?"

Ida nodded. The apartment was silent. Muffled traffic noises and occasional cries could be heard from the street. Ida made as if to leave the room, turned back again and said, touching her forehead: "You know, signora, people tell me things and I worry about them. What can I do about it? I do worry so."

6

The signora looked at her and asked: "But what's happened?"

Ida wrung her rather stumpy hands together and said: "That was my sister Giulia on the phone. She told me that her former boy-friend has turned up again, nearly a year after he'd left her. He's called Nando. And she forgives him, they're getting together again."

The signora took her mind back to that sister of Ida's whom she'd met only once. She'd come to pick up Ida one Sunday afternoon. She was a tiny wisp of a girl, but had beautiful eyes, brimming with light. She'd held out her hand diffidently. She had a husky voice but spoke good Italian with almost aggressive assurance. The signora opened out her hands and replied: "Well, let her be. After all, Giulia's older than you are."

Ida jibbed slightly and said forcefully: "But then she shouldn't tell me all about it, she ought to leave me in peace." She pressed her throat and red patches immediately appeared. She shook her head and said: "I don't want to go through everything with Giulia all over again. Believe me, you can't get any peace with her. She'll say one thing while she's thinking another, she's difficult, I don't understand her." She lowered her voice and whispered without looking at the signora: "When Nando dropped her a year ago, she tried to kill herself."

The signora was shaken, she could see Giulia's tight little face and murmured: "Oh, my God, how terrible. Who would have thought it?"

Ida was standing still in front of her. Her legs felt like lead, she glanced at the armchair but did not dare sit down. Her mind was full of images of the hospital at night, with those dismal shaded lights and her sister, so tiny and frenzied and all strapped down.

"Yes, she attempted it," she repeated rapidly. "Giulia and I were serving the same family. For some time Nando had been acting strangely, threatening to leave her and then come back again. Giulia was hardly eating a thing, and morning and evening, at any and at every moment, she kept saying to me: I'll kill myself, I'll kill myself. I kept talking to her about our mother, sobbing and pleading with her. One day I even told our *padrona* that Giulia was saying this, that and the other, and that she ought to be careful, but she told

7

me: Go on, people who keep saying things never do them, your sister just reads too many photo-romances. That evening I'd gone to lend a hand at the signora's mother's where there was going to be a party, and Giulia had stayed at home alone, saying, I've a headache, I'm going to sleep. A few hours later, while we were over there, the house-porter rang to say that we must rush over straight away because Giulia had poisoned herself. The signori took her to hospital where they cleaned out her stomach: only just in time, that's what they said, only just in time. I never left her side. I never moved from her bed that whole night or the following day or the second night and I just cried and cried and cried. I couldn't bear the thought that my sister could have done anything like that. I sat there on that little chair beside her bed, and seeing her so little and white and all strapped up, my God, I kept thinking of my father and mother and I felt responsible for what she had done and I could see them before my eyes asking: Why weren't you watching over your sister? And I kept thinking about when all four of us sisters were little, and Giulia was such a mite and wasn't strong enough to do anything, and my father shouted at her for not being strong enough and even I, who was younger, was better than her at everything. And when she started talking on the second night, as she was returning to her senses, I asked her: Giulia, why did you do it? Because of Nando? Because of Nando? And she kept sighing and saying: Yes, on account of him, and on account of lots of things I can't explain, I was so tired and I couldn't face carrying on. So we were both weeping together, do you see, signora? God, what I went through. Even the doctor, the one in charge of my sister, was alarmed by the state I was in, and every time he visited the ward he had an injection given to me as well and kept telling me: Don't you cry, you sister's a nitwit, you just can't behave like that. And when we left the hospital he had a word with the signora and told her that I was over-sensitive, that girls shouldn't be sent into service at fourteen, and he advised her to watch me too."

She stood there, features drawn, red eyes staring. Then her thoughts switched to her mother. She could see her before her eyes, sharply defined yet distant at the same time, her face small and mournful, her dress black. She pulled back her headscarf that had slipped forward over her forehead, placed her hand on her chest where she could feel her heart pounding and murmured: "So, do you see, signora?"

The signora made a movement and the newspaper rustled to the floor. She stooped to pick it up and didn't know what to say.

"What's wrong?"

"Nothing."

"What did the doctor say?"

"That I'm too thin. That I must have some injections. But I won't."

"Why not?"

"Because I'm scared."

"No one can be scared of injections."

"I am."

"What else did the doctor say?"

"That I have bad nerves and low blood-pressure."

The signora put her hand on her forehead and said: "You must have the injections. Do you understand?"

"I won't. I'm scared."

"You're not a child, you can't talk like that."

"I won't have them. I've already told the doctor I won't."

The signora turned her back on her and said: "You're silly. Don't you complain if you don't feel well."

Ida started noisily on her chores. She tramped in and out of the kitchen with her eyes lowered. She picked up the linen-basket and went out to hang up the washing. Her hands and wrists looked large in relation to her body, which had become skinnier and almost knobbly. The signora went after her and asked brusquely: "Well, what is it? Is anything else the matter?"

"No, nothing."

"But what the devil's wrong with you?"

Ida did not reply. She kept her eyes lowered and her face and temples were flushed in streaks. She thought: I'll leave, I'll hand in my notice. I can't stand her any more. There are so many other domestic posts in Rome, it's just a matter of picking one. She pictured herself wandering through the streets of Rome, so immense and thronged with crowds of people going this way and that, this way and that, that sometimes it gave her a feeling resembling nausea and she had to clutch at the walls of houses to prop herself up and wait until she recovered. She pictured herself ringing a doorbell, and when the door opened she'd say the usual things and the unknown family would eye her up and down, interrogate her. She thought: I'll go back home. If I really want to, I can easily go back to our village, to my mother's. She saw the familiar fields and country lanes and her mother sitting on the doorstep, tiredness in her eyes, her hands joined on her lap. She frowned and gasped: "Oh."

The signora gave her a vexed look. "Aren't you well?" she asked. "If you aren't, look after yourself. Have those injections, and let that be the end of it. Right?"

Ida did not reply. Grey shadows spread around her eyes, over her temples and down to her cheeks. She stood there, deep in thought yet tense, as if vibrating inwardly. Looking at her, the signora softened and repeated: "Do you understand, Ida?"

"Yes, yes," answered Ida. "I understand perfectly."

She turned her back on her and escaped to her room. She drew down the roller-blind, flung her pillow against the wall, lay back on the bed and stared up at the ceiling in the penumbra.

The signora glanced through the drawers and shelves and made a note of what was needed. Then she went out. She walked swiftly, looking around, the cars, the people, watching out for something that might engage her attention. Her back was aching, she felt bad and terribly insecure.

She was back very soon with a full carrier-bag, put it on the kitchen table and called: "Ida."

The girl appeared in the doorway. The signora studied her and asked: "Are you better?"

Ida shook her head. The signora took a deep breath and went on: "You can't carry on like this. Don't you realize I want to help you?"

Ida shook her head again. There was a darkness filled with flashes in her eyes. The signora cried: "Oh, my God, I can't go on feeling like this on account of you."

Ida turned her back on her and said: "Don't look at me, don't speak to me. It's as if I didn't exist. Just let me be."

A great bouquet of flowers arrived, the signora smiled with pleasure and arranged them in the vase. She smoothed out the creases in the table-cloth and adjusted a wine-glass here, a knife or a spoon there.

"Not a word about the cake," she said, as she went past the kitchen. "It's a surprise."

Her husband arrived and said: "Happy birthday." They embraced.

Her son got back from school and immediately called out: "Happy birthday, happy birthday." They sat down to table and started the meal. Ida rushed to and fro between kitchen and dining-room a trifle breathlessly and haphazardly as usual, to the signora's annoyance, but a smoother service seemed impossible to achieve. Everybody had stories to tell and things to laugh at, and from time to time the signora would touch her son's or her husband's hand and say: Yes, of course, yes. Ida carried in the cake with pink candles on and she too said: "Happy birthday, signora."

The signora smiled and replied: "Sit down with us. We must all have some cake together."

"No, no," said Ida, blushing. "It's all right."

The boy cried, "Come on, fetch yourself a plate and sit down."

Ida gave him a friendly glance, took a dessert-plate from the trolley and moved towards the chair, but did not sit down.

"Sit down," said the boy, "come along, sit down."

Ida sat down side on, blushed again high up on her cheeks and her eyes shone vividly. She kept still, though a little excited, and when her turn came she cut herself a sliver and remarked genteelly: "It should be good, judging by its appearance."

She at the first few morsels, glanced about her and began again, all animation: "You're not all that fond of sweet dishes are you? Pity, I can make some good ones. At signora Terzi's I learnt to make tarts and profiteroles and trifles, though my trifle is a bit different from the usual, I add some ingredients of my own. I don't look at cookery books, or if I do, I adapt, I invent my own recipes and my dishes always turn out all right, they do, don't they?"

The signora concurred, "Yes, yes."

The boy said: "I've got to get back to school, we're having an assembly."

"But when do you learn anything?" asked his mother. She glanced at her husband, who appeared preoccupied, laid her napkin on the table and, rising briskly to her feet, ordered: "And now, Ida, you make us some good coffee."

Ida took her coat and stood in the middle of the room in her short skirt that left more of her legs bare, legs that were strong in the calf but slender in the thigh, giving her a somewhat graceless air. The signora looked at her and was impelled to enquire: "So – how are you getting on with your boyfriend?"

Ida arched her eyebrows and said: "Fine. How do you expect us to get on? Fine."

Her face was pale and her eyes had dark rings and a deep, melancholy look.

The signora thought for a moment about her own younger days and persisted: "But do you feel sure? Do you see eye to eye?"

"Yes, yes," replied Ida. "Pietro is a sensible fellow. He already often makes plans for when we're married. He asks me what nice dishes I can cook and whether I can make *orecchiette* pasta. He says that when we have a house we'll have two television sets, a big one in the dining-room and a smaller one in the bedroom, like his married sister. In fact the one in the dining-room is hardly ever on because he says it's much better to stay in bed to watch television."

"But you must talk about other things as well, surely?"

"Certainly. Pietro says that when we get married he wants to have an American-style kitchen with all the facilities, including a roasting-spit. He's very thrifty. He never throws money away, even though everything is still a long way off as he has to do his military service and then a relative has promised to get him a job in telephone maintenance, which would be excellent, wouldn't it?"

The signora gave Ida a searching look and could not help saying: "You have such a way of talking."

Ida gave a toss of her head, looked out of the window and mumbled: "The sun's out again."

The signora continued with a hint of reproach: "You're so young. I feel people shouldn't be like that at your age."

Ida broke in: "But it's all so far away. Still, Pietro says that in order to get ready for marriage and have everything you need you must have money and so he's already saving from now. And then he says he's also saving on my behalf, because I have to send money to my parents and I have nothing left to put aside. Isn't that right, signora?"

"Yes, certainly," answered the signora. She thought: Poor Ida, I want to give her something one of these days. She sighed and a question suddenly occurred to her: "But Pietro – do you love him? Are you in love?"

Ida opened her eyes wide, little black specks swam in her iris; she lowered her eyes and said slowly: "And why would I stay with him if not? At first I wasn't in love, you're right. Now I'm attached to him and I miss him if he's not around."

Ida entered the house, the door slipped from her grasp and slammed shut noisily. "Sorry," she cried. And then: "Where are you? Where are you, signora? Ah, here you are."

She went up to her, smiling, and she looked pretty, her complexion fine and rosy, and she announced: "Do you know, signora? On Sunday, Pietro's taking me to see his mother."

"Haven't you met her yet?" the signora asked in amazement.

Ida shook her head and went on quickly, "Pietro says he wanted to prime her, to tell her about me. So when we meet, she'll already know me. Pietro is the only son, he's his mother's favourite."

The girl slowly removed her short, deep-red coat, toyed with her keys and said, hesitantly but gaily: "What do you say, signora? Will I appeal to Pietro's mother?"

The signora contemplated her smilingly for an instant and said: "I really think you will."

Ida heaved a long breath and mumbled: Let's hope so,

let's hope so. She made for the kitchen but before leaving the room said aloud: "I want to buy her a present. I'm not going to see her empty-handed."

"You'd best take her some flowers," replied the signora. "Being the first time."

Ida turned round and said, "A nice plant, then. Why not an azalea?"

The signora smiled to herself and reflected that Ida was always wanting to give presents and that when she was buying a present expense was no object and it was she who had to tell her: now don't exaggerate, after all you have to work hard for what you earn.

"Well, did it go all right?"

Ida raised her shining eyes and nodded affirmatively. She was silent for some minutes, then ran after the signora and said: "It went fine. I've got her on my side, I think."

"Pietro's mother?"

"Yes, yes, I've got her on my side. Don't laugh, signora. It was difficult at first, Pietro wouldn't help me, he just stood there goggling like a fish, and his mother, too, stared at me and wouldn't say a word and I talked and talked and didn't even know what I was saying. But it went fine."

"I'm glad," said the signora.

"I'm glad, too. Very, very glad. I was scared, you know. Last night I couldn't sleep for worrying, but now I feel easy" – and she took two steps towards the signora and looked more peaceful than usual.

The signora enquired, coming up to Ida: "And what is his mother like?"

"She resembles Pietro, but is heavier. But she dresses well, you can see she sets store by that. In the end she was smiling, she seemed a different woman. Perhaps she was shy or embarrassed and thawed out little by little as she looked at me and listened to me. Perhaps she thought Pietro had taken up with a different kind of girl, you know what I mean?"

She ran to her room and came back almost directly with a red scarf.

14

"She gave me this," she said. "She told me: you must have something from me, young lady." She tossed the scarf around her neck and went on: "It's warm, you know. And red does suit me. Doesn't it suit me, signora?"

She glanced at the signora and then immediately looked at herself in the gilt hall mirror: the signora also looked in the mirror, which reflected their two faces smiling side by side.

The signora entered Ida's room where the ironing-board was set up in one corner. Ida was behind the board, bent forward, and was taking short, heavy sweeps at a man's shirt with the clothes-iron. The signora watched, then said: "If you're tired, leave it. You can do the ironing tomorrow."

Ida shook her head and replied: "Now, now, don't say that. You know I've got things to do."

"Is something bothering you?"

Ida didn't answer. She was very pale, and her transparent eyelids looked blue. She put down the iron, folded the shirt and said with a profound sigh. "Sometimes I'd like to go far away where nobody knows me. Perhaps some day I will, I'll take my suitcase and make off. I'll disappear."

The signora smiled at the image as one does with children and asked: "What's happened?"

Ida shrugged and said· "People just don't understand. They torment me."

"Who's tormenting you?"

"Everybody. But they just don't understand a thing. Not even Pietro and his friends."

"And why do they torment you?"

Ida looked out of the window, which was smaller than the usual size and displayed only a strip of blue, and said, still gazing out: "You've no idea. It's on account of the work I do here."

"Your work?"

Ida flushed and a little sweat stood out on her skin. "But what do I do?" she said. "Why should I be ashamed? I work. I earn my living as I can."

The signora murmured: "Of course, that's right."

Ida arranged the shirts in a row, unplugged the iron and

said: "I need a short rest."

She sat on her small bed and clutched her head between her hands. The signora leaned against the door and repeatedly patiently: "What's wrong, Ida? Go on, tell me about it?"

Ida raised her eyes. She had a bewildered look. "Oh," she said, "what I can't bear is that even Pietro is the same as the others, he doesn't understand a thing, just like his stupid friends and relatives. Do you know what he had the face to tell me? That this job – the work I do here for you – is not at all to his liking. Or his mother's, D'you hear, signora – his mother's? 'But didn't she meet me?' I asked. 'Didn't she say I'm a sensible girl?' 'Yes, yes,' he replied, 'but it's your work she disapproves of and she says you ought to change jobs, find something different, because it embarrasses her.'"

Ida had raised her voice, anguish flashed in her eyes. She looked at the signora and asked: "But what will that change, I ask. What difference will it make? Say I become a shop-assistant? Where am I going to live? Who's going to support me? Who'll send money home? And if I don't, what are my parents and my little sister going to live on? But Pietro doesn't understand, because someone who lives with his own family can't understand. He can't have any idea of what it means to arrive in Rome at the age of fourteen all by yourself." She pressed her chest and throat, took a deep breath and, her eyes filling with tears, resumed: "I'm amazed at Pietro's mother, who's a mature woman and still doesn't understand a thing. Face to face, she talked affectionately to me, but she didn't mean any of it. And I've been nice to her and I've done all Pietro asked of me so as to please her. And then she goes behind my back saying she's embarrassed by the job I'm doing and Pietro backs her up. What have I done wrong? Tell me, signora, what is there to be ashamed about in what I'm doing?"

The signora avoided the girl's gaze, she laid her hand on her arm and said gently: "Keep calm. It was stupid of them to talk like that. Very stupid." She turned about, took a couple of steps, stopped again and repeated: "Put it out of your mind. You'll see, everything will sort itself out."

She felt heavy-headed and went to her room. She sat down on the edge of her bed and picked up a book, but her thoughts were elsewhere.

Upon her return from a trip with her husband, the signora took the household in hand again, absent-mindedly checked through the bills, heard all her son's news about school and friends and finally asked Ida: "Have you any news?"

"No," said Ida, looking at the ground. Then she turned red, two long tears coursed down her cheeks and she said in a low voice: "Pietro's left me."

The signora looked at her in disbelief and exclaimed: "He can't have! Pietro, your boy-friend. Whatever happened?"

She thought for a moment about all the problems of being young and sighed: Poor Ida, whatever happened?

Ida hastily wiped away her tears and replied: "I don't want to talk about it. It's all over, and that's it."

The signora was not really displeased by Ida's reserve, so she said: "I just wanted to help you. I really wasn't expecting that." She was silent for a moment, then added: "But Pietro, he seemed so much in love, didn't he?"

Ida made a vague gesture and went over to the window. She closed the shutters, as evening had fallen, turned on the lights and mumbled: "I'm going into the kitchen."

The signora approached her, stopped her and, resting her hand on the girl's shoulder, said: "I do hope you don't take it too much to heart. You're still so young."

The girl abruptly bent down her head and murmured: "You'd only just left when it happened. I've got over the worst."

The signora could not work out whether Pietro was in an emotional state or whether it was his Apulian accent that made him gobble his words. He had a handsome Southern face with high cheek-bones and gentle, black eyes and only when he spoke could you see his strong but uneven teeth.

He said: "Ida sent word she won't see me and I don't know what to make of it. So I've come to you, signora, perhaps you can tell me something."

The signora shook her head; she was surprised and

17

embarrassed and replied slowly: "I don't know anything exactly. I thought it was you that had broken off with Ida."

Pietro's expression was one of astonishment mixed with disbelief: "What are you saying, signora? I love that girl, and I can't get over it. Because no one can live all by himself, what's the point of living without the thought that you love someone and that someone loves you? At first she told me: 'I don't think I'm in love, I don't know what I feel.' Then she did come to love me, I'm sure of that. But what's really going on inside her is beyond me. You enquire, you search, but it's like talking to a wall. She won't say anything, or if she does she says things you just can't believe."

The signora rose, poured him a drink and said: "You're both so young, you've got so much life ahead of you: give Ida time to think it over. Maybe she'll change her mind."

Pietro downed his drink and said quickly: "But it upsets me to be without her. I go home, I go to my married sister's, I nip round to the bar, but I don't speak, I'm withdrawn, I keep thinking that if she were with me everything would be different. Will you tell her all this?"

The signora could not restrain herself from smiling slightly, though sympathetically, and replied: "Yes, of course, I'll tell her everything."

"You must tell her that I'm waiting for her. Because I appreciate that girl and I'm willing to make a lot of sacrifices for her. You don't know me, signora, but I've thought seriously about every step I've taken."

The signora looked at the sky, the trees outside the window, because the boy's words and his expression on his face were so intense they made her feel uncomfortable. She said gently: "Don't worry, I'll tell Ida everything. But don't expect too much. As you've realized yourself, Ida hasn't got a simple character."

She rose, intimating to the young man that she had no more time to spare. When Pietro had gone, she remained seated in her armchair, half sighing over the whole thing and half laughing.

The signora let some days go by, being occupied with other matters and ill-at-ease about intruding into Ida's sentimental affairs. On her way home she caught a glimpse of Pietro gazing at their window from the pavement opposite and she decided to raise the matter.

She summoned Ida into the study and eyed her carefully for a moment.

"What is it?" asked Ida. "What do you want, signora?"

The signora replied, irritated: "Why did you tell me a lie? Pietro was here last Sunday and told me it was you that left him."

Ida bit her lip, avoided the signora's gaze, and retorted: "Me, him, what difference does it make? The fact remains, we're no longer together."

"Why leave him? He's a good lad, he loves you deeply. You'll have an untroubled life with him."

Ida shrugged her shoulders and replied: "I don't in the least care about an untroubled life or that there's some money in the family. That's what I've decided and I'm better off this way."

The signora recalled with some fondness what Pietro had said, his stammering and mumbling, and said: "This is no way to behave. Pietro is in despair, you should at least talk to him."

"In due course," said Ida. "For the time being I don't want to see either of them, either him or his mother."

"How does his mother come into it?" asked the signora, taken aback. "How does she come into it?"

Ida shook her head, her gaze moved away and she muttered: "She has nothing to do with it, I'm going back to the kitchen, I have work to do."

The signora resumed putting her papers in order, but her mind was still on the business of Ida, which she was unable to fathom. When Ida reappeared with some dishes, she addressed her: "I will have to say something to Pietro. What am I to report?"

Ida stood in the middle of the living-room, she was extremely pale and had rings round her eyes. She answered: "I've already told you – that I don't want to see them again. I don't need them."

The signora went on looking through her papers while she pursued an idea that had suddenly struck her. She left her desk, moved towards Ida and said: "Do you know what I think? That you're taking revenge on Pietro and particularly on his mother."

The girl made a gesture as if to say: what nonsense.

"But that's it. You want to avenge yourself, cause that lad to suffer: on account of what they said about your working here, about being embarrassed."

Ida reddened and broke in: "But what are you thinking of? It's not as you say."

"Well, how is it, then?"

"It's something else." She looked away, far away, her eyes glistening. She said slowly, almost syllable by syllable: "Yes, I don't like Pietro's mother, I admit that. But it's not on account of that woman that I'm dropping Pietro. I'm no longer interested in him, that's all." She looked at the signora almost smiling as she said: "I'm no longer interested in him. Beside me, Pietro was like a child and I felt he was beneath me."

The signora was dumbfounded, thought of the boy and murmured: "But what are you saying?"

Ida had recovered her assurance and replied: "I'm telling you what I think. When we were together he was like a child and it was useless to tell him: Pietro, stop, you're tiring me out. Besides, other people, too, realized that I was better than him. Poor Pietro, it really is all over."

"I'm worried about Diana," Ida said suddenly, "you know, signora? – Diana, the Levas' girl, on the second floor, she disappeared two days ago. The Levas came to ask me if I knew anything about it. It's a problem for them when Diana doesn't turn up because they have no one to look after the baby."

"Don't you know where she lives?" asked the signora. "Haven't the Levas got her address?"

"Sure," said Ida, "but there's nobody at home and the neighbours couldn't tell them anything." Ida lowered her eyes, began to strain the cooked vegetables and whispered: "I can tell you, signora. Diana's having an abortion."

The signora sat down and said: "Poor thing, who knows

in whose hands she's landed herself."

Ida resumed in a louder voice: "I don't know where she is, they wouldn't tell me. Besides, she says she's used to it, she's done it before. But I'm worried, I can't help thinking about it. She isn't a bad girl, you know? She's very kind, in fact. Whenever she comes to see me, she always brings me some sweets or pastries and tells me about herself. She hasn't been back home for years, they hardly ever exchange letters and she's alone here in Rome, there's no one with her."

"Poor thing," repeated the signora and pictured to herself Diana's plump, regular face.

Ida set aside the vegetable purée, leaned upon the formica-topped table and said: "For years she's had a fellow, she often mentions him and speaks well of him. But I've formed a different impression of him and I think that man's using her. They quarrel, they fight, they split up, but Diana can't manage on her own, she seeks out new company right away, especially young fellows, I think she likes young fellows." She gave a mischievous little smile, hesitated, then continued: "You have no idea of the life which Diana and her sort lead. They stay up very late at night, go out to bars, drink, go out driving and sometimes, so she tells me, one of them suddenly says: Shall we go over to L'Aquila? Shall we drive to Naples for a coffee? So they race around like lunatics and don't even get to bed because by the time they've got back it's already time for them to go to work. Or else they go up to Diana's, as she's got a self-contained room, and make love there, all together, without any shame at all. Just lately Diana's been very tired all the time and during the day she always had a splitting headache and was ready to drop for lack of sleep. A few days ago she was in the park with the Levas' baby girl and fell asleep on the bench. She was fast asleep for two hours. When she woke up she had a terrible fright and began sobbing and crying out, but fortunately she found the little girl playing a little way off. It shook her, though, because she's a decent sort."

"Good God," said the signora, shaking her head. "You can't be that irresponsible at her age. Just think what might have happened." She stood up and said, preoccupied: "And perhaps you'd better not see her too often."

Ida lowered her gaze, gestured vaguely and replied: "I

think she's most unhappy. She's no longer young, she isn't content with her job, but couldn't take on anything else, not anything."

A few days later, the signora met Diana on the stairs of the apartment block. She'd lost weight and her face looked small and pinched.

"Good day, signora," the other greeted her first.

"Good day," replied the signora. She felt an impulse, for a moment considered approaching her and talking to her, but it was awkward and in the end she just passed by.

"Would you like a book?"

Ida made a negative gesture and stared at the bookshelves arching her eyebrows.

"Why don't you read?"

"I don't know."

"You ought to read. And you ought to look around you, Ida. You ought to participate more in the world."

"Do you think so?"

Ida sighed, shook her head and, looking dully at the signora, said: "Perhaps you're right, signora. Sometimes I myself feel I'd like to take interest in all the things you talk about with your husband and your son. And I've tried picking up a book, your son's given me some. But after I've been reading for a while I realize that I don't care one bit about all that writing and my thoughts wander off again on their own." She took a couple of steps towards the signora and continued: "I've received a letter from Germany. It's from my cousin, he went to work there but hasn't found a job. He'd like to come back but he hasn't enough money for the journey because before leaving he'd only saved enough for the outward journey. I'm so sorry for him, if only you could see him: he's short, he only comes up to here and he has an ulcer and suffers from headaches."

"But is he on his own in Germany?"

"His wife had joined him at one time, but then she had a baby and didn't want to go back there. And to think that the people in my village don't think it's so bad to go away, after all, they say, people have always done that and you've got to grin and bear it."

The signora was listening with interest. She asked, "Does he speak German at least?"

"Just a few words." Ida drew form her pocket a sheet of lined paper and said quickly: "Would you like to hear what he wrote me at the end of his letter? 'My dear cousin, after so many months of toil away from home, I long continuously for only one thing – to return to our village. I know that once I'm back there everything will be difficult for me as it was before and that I won't solve the problem of our livelihood. But you cannot imagine how I feel here every hour of the day; I really feel I don't belong to anybody without my dear wife and child.' "

The signora entered the kitchen in some excitement and said: "Ida, I've been thinking things over these last few days. You can't carry on like this."

"How do you mean, like this?"

"Without prospects, without any idea for your future. I've given it a lot of thought. You're young, you're bright, it's crazy that you shouldn't try something different. You can sign up for a course in typing plus something else, we could discuss what. I'm finding out about it, it isn't difficult."

Ida smiled incredulously, made a sweeping gesture that included the whole apartment and said: "But what are you saying? What about the house-work?"

"Don't worry about your duties just now," replied the signora. "You'll take a bit less time over them. Count yourself free from three o'clock and get everything done by that time."

Ida shook her head and objected: "Even though I passed my third-form exams, I remember so little. Every year that goes by for me is like two or three years, I remember the names of the things I've learnt, but not where they belong. The same with spelling."

The signora interrupted and replied firmly: "I'll help you, I know how. I do have some experience, you'll see." She laughed happily at her plan and added tongue-in-cheek: "I have every confidence in your intelligence, Ida, and I'm sure you can do it."

Ida reddened slightly and her eyes shone. She mused a while, then said slowly: "I don't know what to think, it sounds so crazy. Do you really think it will help? That I might change?"

"Yes, I do. And in any case it will be good for you, it will get you out of here, give you something different to do. You're so young, you have so many opportunities." And as she said this the signora cast an uncertain backward glance over the past, but she recovered herself and added: "I would really like to help you."

Ida nodded, a happy look came over her face, but it darkened suddenly and she said: "But what about my parents? What will they say?"

"They'll be pleased."

Ida shook her head repeatedly and blurted: "I don't think so, in fact I'm sure they won't."

"And why not?"

"They don't want anything to change. For them things are fine the way they are, with me here sending money home, the way they've always been."

The signora started with astonishment and almost cried out: "But you'll be studying to improve your situation."

"They don't understand these things."

The signora disguised her dismay and simply said: "Don't you worry, I'll write to your parents. I'll explain to them that you won't be risking anything because you'll still be with us while you're studying."

Ida returned from typing school in great excitement. She put down her text-book and work-book, took off her light-coloured velvet jacket that set off her thick chestnut hair and said: "I feel I'm a little girl at school again."

"Good," said the signora, "I'm glad."

Ida went up to her and said: "I enjoyed going to school,

24

you know? In fact the reason why I have my middle school certificate is that my class-mistress told my parents, Make sure she studies, she's brighter than her sisters, she might be able to carry on. But my parents wouldn't hear of it because in our parts things aren't the same they are over here, where families value learning even if they're not educated like you and your husband. When we were little we were always left alone during the day, my mother and father were out in the fields working. They got up before dawn and rushed off without preparing any food for us. So I and my sisters, getting back from school, would take a piece of bread and cheese and wander round the house like stray kittens nibbling away at the bread." She reddened and went on hastily: "I don't remember ever sitting down to a hot meal on coming back from school. Sometimes I and my sisters would say: Come on, let's go over to uncle's, perhaps they'll give us something nice to eat, and we'd go as far as their house and say: Has Matri left a message for us? We'd say that so as not to let on that we'd gone to see them in the hopes of getting some hot soup. And our uncle and aunt would often reply: Come on, stay here with us, and they'd give us some soup. I expect this all sounds funny to you, signora, doesn't it?"

The signora indicated that it did not, gave a half-sigh and said: "Not at all. I was just thinking about your mother, who couldn't find even a little bit of time to be with you."

Ida interrupted quickly: "But on Sundays she always prepared everything properly, table-cloth and all, you mustn't think she didn't like cooking, but on every other day she got up so early and went out with my father to the fields which were far from our house and did a man's work. It was evening by the time they returned home and they were both so tired, especially my mother, who would fling herself on to a chair and rest her head on the table, so it would be up to us children to put the pot on the fire and prepare a hot meal."

"Yes, yes, we spoke Sardinian at home, but not all the time. We spoke Sardinian with the old folk because my grandmother, for example, couldn't speak Italian, she really

25

didn't know any, couldn't even understand it. But we often spoke to my father in Italian, he did his military service in the north of Italy and so he said that we had to learn Italian properly and that Sardinian was no use at all. Here in Rome, I and my sisters talk Sardinian amongst ourselves now. I remember Rosa and I once starting off, Come on, let's talk Sardinian, and we were all excited and we talked so much and it felt so lovely. All at once we're stuck for a word, just an ordinary word, we can't remember how to say 'bat', and we feel we just can't have completely forgotten the word, so we both think about it as hard as we can, almost in tears on account of not being able to recall this word that we must have used to many, many times and I don't know what we did to try and remember it. And suddenly it comes back to me and I say it and Rosa repeats it and it's as if something beautiful has happened and we're laughing over it and half crying. That was just how it was, you know, signora? We kept laughing and half crying and say that word over and over. What nitwits, eh?"

"And what is the word for bat?" asked the signora. "How do you say it in Sardinian?"

"A-le e ped-de," replied Ida. "We say a-le e ped-de."

"A-le e ped-de?" repeated the signora.

"Yes, but we pronounce it differently,' Ida explained. "A-le e ped-de: d'you hear it?"

The signora smiled and said, "Yes, yes." She left the kitchen but went on thinking about that curious story.

"Tacque?"
"C-Q, right?"
"Taccuino?"
"Double C."
"Taceremo?"
"One C and one M."
"Taceremmo?"
"Double M?"
"Tappeto?"
"Double T?"
"No, double P and one T."

"Scatola?"

"Oh, I give up."

The boy came in in high spirits and cried, "Olio? Oglio? Aglio? Giglio? Guglielmo?"

Ida tittered and covered her face with her hands: "Give over, for goodness' sake, my head's splitting."

"But you've been making progress," said the boy, "I've been noticing."

Ida gave him an affectionate look and said: "At times I say to myself: All the time I've wasted. At other times, on the contrary, I think: All this fag won't get me anywhere and I'll always be stuck doing homework." And she glanced down at the floor, which was the principal object of her labours. Then she continued: "Last night I was perusing the dictionary you gave me, right up to midnight and later. In the end the words were whirling round in a muddle inside my head and I couldn't take in another thing."

The boy came back: "I'm certain you'll cope. You've no idea how ignorant people are." He pondered a moment and then turned to his mother and said, "Really and truly, schooling nowadays is only of value to Ida and people like her, don't you think?"

So mother and son left the room, the mother holding her son by the arm, and they talked together about the problems in schools, which at that time were being swept by the protest movement.

"I was on my own in Rome when I was fourteen. When I arrived I didn't even have a dress, only the one I was wearing. The signori I was working for weren't bad, but often quarrelled, the signora was even hard on her children who were always crying and running to me for comfort. The youngest became so fond of me, he'd never leave me and sometimes he'd even come and slip into bed with me and wouldn't get out again, but if the signora noticed she'd get more cross with me than with him. I didn't know what to do on Sundays. The signori would go and see their relatives, my sisters Rosa and Giulia didn't want to have me in their way because they already had boy-friends, so I'd get on a bus and do the whole journey, all the way to the terminus and back again, and then go back home, and I'd often cry in the street without even knowing why. Just think, at the age of fourteen I was earning thirty thousand lira per month, and I'd send twenty thousand home and keep five thousand for myself. As I wrote home every day, my five thousand lira all went on postage. I remember the first postal draft I sent: a hundred thousand lira, all I'd earned since I entered service three months earlier."

She was silent for a moment, her eyes had turned grey and she was gazing over the signora's head. She said: "What parents I had. To send me off like that to Rome at fourteen, straight from a little village. Imagine – before then, I hadn't even been to Cagliari."

At the Supermarket the signora bought some jam which as usual she'd forgotten to get earlier. She would often forget to buy something or other, then think better of it and run back at the last moment to make good the oversight and make sure nothing was lacking at home. At the cash-desk she opened her purse and saw that the amount of money was different from what she had put there a short while before. She immediately had the sensation that somebody had been rummaging in her hand-bag and felt that that sensation had come to her several times lately, but she hadn't paid any attention to it.

She returned home and did her sums again. She found the original supermarket check, counted the amounts and the change and jotted down on a scrap of paper everything she'd done between her first and second visit to the supermarket. She tried to remember every step she'd made, which she found highly uncongenial. She found she was seven thousand lira short. She was sure of it, almost. But she refused to think it was Ida.

Nevertheless, that evening she decided to carry out an experiment. She was almost certain she'd got things wrong and that she'd had a mental blank, which often happened to her, but she wanted to dispel the doubt that had been nagging her during the day. She and her husband counted up her money and both noted the amount left in her purse. They exchanged uneasy glances, but said: the experiment will show there's nothing wrong, but it's better to go through with it so as not to be in any doubt and also because neither of them was ever very careful about checking how much money they left lying around the house in pockets and handbags. It's such a nuisance to have to keep thinking about money, but it has to be done.

The following morning, three one-thousand lira notes were missing. They ascertained that this was the case and hardly exchanged a word on the matter. The signora saw that Ida had already started tidying up the living-room, looked at her with changed eyes, avoided saying anything to her and went out quickly. She walked a little way from home, pained at everything that had happened. She kept saying to herself: Who would ever have thought it? She steals, she pilfers. And she visualized her in the act of glancing around and opening the handbag. She's a thief, she thought, and crafty, too. Who knows how long she's been at it, perhaps right from the start. All day long that thought was in her head, she couldn't get rid of it, and she noticed that a new feeling was taking shape inside her, almost of relief, a subtle satisfaction, even, because that figure was now looming less large, not getting so much under her skin. She wondered how she ought to behave. She tried imagining the things she might say to Ida, but as she searched for things to say she realized she didn't want to tackle her and that everything that came into her head was foolish. She also threw her mind back to certain temptations she herself had experienced as a girl, which somewhat disturbed her. In the end she decided that for that day, at least, she would do nothing. She thought: I'll be more careful and perhaps she'll work things out for herself.

Ida went on following classes in the afternoon. She was now also following a course in machine graphics, a new subject of which the signora knew nothing at all. In the morning Ida would show her the punched cards she had done the day before and explain how the machine worked. She would say: "It isn't as hard as it looks. I manage quite well. I really feel I'm making progress."

One morning she approached the signora's bed holding a bunch of cards and said: "Do you know, signora? I'm the best. The head of department told me so yesterday. She said: Ida, you're the best of the trainees, if we exclude Bruna, who's already in employment and is following the course just by way of brushing up. Splendid, isn't it? I'm pleased, very, very pleased." She smiled and her eyes grew large and filled with light. "I'll get the diploma, just think!" She thrust her head forward a little, like a donkey, and laughed: "Who knows, I might still become somebody, what do you say, signora?"

The signora agreed, and replied: "You're intelligent. If you apply yourself, you'll succeed in whatever you do."

Ida reflected, sighed and said, "I'm not sure I'm as intelligent as you say. At school I was good at maths. But I was weak in Italian, my essays didn't turn out well."

"Did you make many mistakes?"

"Yes, it was on account of my mistakes that I got bad marks. Not on account of my ideas. In fact my essays were sometimes read out in class for the content. I remember one of my essays which was read out and my form-mistress kept saying: Well done, well done, and she even showed it to her colleagues. The title was *Write about someone who is dear to you*."

"And who did you write about?"

Ida smiled faintly, looked into the distance with an intense light in her eyes. She said: "My mother."

And she stayed stock still, pursuing who knows what thoughts and memories, and the signora recalled to her mind's eye the short woman so full of dignity and severity whom she had met a year earlier.

The signora was pottering about in the garden, Ida came out of the kitchen and asked her: "What are you doing?"

The signora, who was removing dead leaves from the geraniums and did that sort of thing listlessly, sensed a touch of irony and replied: "Nothing. Go and get lunch ready."

Ida went off and the signora had a look at the plants, the fine persimmon full of golden fruit, but quickly came away and also entered the house by way of the kitchen. Her bag, slung from the back of a chair, was swinging, and Ida, head bent low, appeared to be arranging the fruit, did not raise her head and was all tense. The signora looked at the girl, snatched up the handbag, went to her own room and began counting her money, but found herself unable to think. She was beside herself, returned to the kitchen, replaced something there and said suddenly: "How strange, my accounts don't tally."

Ida reddened till she was almost purple, tears came pouring from her eyes and covered her face and wet her hands and the floor. She gasped and said: "But what are you saying? What d'you suspect me of? I – I who never touch a thing, who have never touched a thing? What are you thinking? What are you driving at? I who'd do anything rather than that."

And the small bent back was shaking with cries and sobs.

The signora looked on in alarm and said quickly: "I'm not thinking anything. Calm yourself. Why are you so agitated?"

Ida threw herself on a chair and went on sobbing.

"Ah," she cried, "I can't carry on, I can't carry on here with you thinking things like that."

The signora interrupted her, raising her voice: "Ida, you must calm yourself. I'm not thinking anything, nothing at all. You know I'm absent-minded. I wasn't getting at you."

Her heart was pounding, she felt upset, and said: "Sit down, have something to drink." Ida sat up, placed her arm on the table and rested her head upon it. The signora touched her on the shoulder and murmured: "Come on, let's calm down. It was a misunderstanding, don't you see? Let's say no more about it."

She walked slowly out of the kitchen, went off to her room and lay down on her bed.

31

On returning home, the signora was struck by Ida's pallor, but said nothing. During the afternoon she saw her go round the house polishing up the silver and brass and her little figure struck her as having lost all its strength. She put down her book and asked: "Is something wrong?"

"It's the same old things on my mind, the same old things," said Ida.

The signora promptly replied, "If you'd like to tell me about them, I might be able to help you."

Ida shook her head and went off holding her polishing cloth. The signora caught up with her and asked once more: "Well, what is it?"

"Nothing," said Ida. "My parents have written to me. They want two hundred thousand lira by Christmas. They've borrowed money and they say I've got to send them that much, they require it by Christmas."

"What about your sisters? And Rosa, who's comfortably off and is married, why doesn't she help them?"

"Because, being married, she's out of it, and Giulia's saving up for her trousseau. That leaves me."

"But these rules of yours are unjust, I can't understand them."

"Yet it's as I say it is. It's always been that way."

A violent downpour began and Ida ran from window to window closing the shutters: "Oh, God," she moaned, "now all the panes are dirty." The rain lashed down, there was a distant rumble and a rattling as of stones against the shutters.

"It's hailing," Ida said loudly. "The garden's white all over, it looks like snow."

The electricity failed and the apartment went dark. The signora started looking for candles, fixed one into the candlestick and lit it.

"That light," said Ida, "I can't bear it. It's so mournful."

The signora looked at her. By that glow she looked tinier and her face longer and marked.

"When I go back home in summer, do you know what I shall do, signora? After I've been there a day or two, I'll put my headcloth on and pull out my old dresses, weird skirts and sweaters from ages ago and I'll go around in that get-up and I won't be a bit bothered any more about being the way I am over here. What of it, signora? If you were to see me there, all slapdash and ugly, you wouldn't recognize me, and so in that state I'll trudge along into the fields at my father's heels, and when I'm there I'll sit down on a stone and think of all the time I've spent there, even minding the sheep. At first in Rome I was ashamed of letting on that I'd minded the sheep, but now I think back to it I don't think it was that bad. How can I explain it to you? You're there all day long, the light changes, the noises change, and after you've been there a while you don't think any more about anything, and it's peaceful, pretty peaceful."

The signora and her son returned from a brief holiday.

"Was it nice?" asked Ida at once. "Did you have fun?"

"Yes, yes," answered the boy. "We saw lots of things."

"Your museums, too?"

"Sure," said the boy. "I've brought you something." And he handed her a little souvenir plate.

Ida was delighted, her eyes turned dark as she said: "You thought of me? I am pleased you thought of me. Thank you."

She went into her room and placed it on her bedside table. Her little room gave on to an inner courtyard, so no noise reached there except the occasional sound of a voice. She stood still and cast a long look all round the room, took a deep breath and went out.

"May I?" she asked, pushing open the bedroom door. "May I come in, signora?"

The signora raised her head and looked at the girl: underneath her apron she was wearing a black sweater that showed up her fair complexion and her fine eyes.

She said: "I have some great news, signora."

"What is it?" asked the signora with interest.

Ida laughed, tossed her head back slightly and said: "Just

33

think: the head of department sent for me and told me that I will easily get through my exams. She even said she would like to help me because I deserve it."

"Excellent," said the signora. "Excellent. You see? You can do it. You're bright."

Ida rocked on her feet and sighed gently. She said, "I'm going back to the kitchen, the joint is on."

A few moments later the signora could hear her going back into the kitchen and resuming her labours. She remained engrossed in thought and tried to visualize the girl's future.

Ida came to her room again and said: "There's something else which I didn't tell you."

"Yes?"

Ida looked out of the window and said quietly: "I'm leaving. I've made arrangements with my cousin, I can stay with them for a while. The head of department told me she's putting me forward for a post and as soon as I've taken my exams I can take it up. And with the balance which you owe me I can get by in the meantime."

"What about your family?"

"My sister Giulia has promised that she will see to them for a few months." She stood staring at a distant point, then said: "I'll leave here in a week's time. I'm leaving next Saturday."

The signora swept her hair back with her hand, then murmured: "Do as you think best. But why didn't you say anything to me?"

Ida did not answer, and left the room. The signora went after her into the kitchen, quite upset, and asked again: "Might I know why you didn't say anything to me?"

Ida pressed her neck with her fingers and red patches appeared. The signora went on sternly: "You haven't been very sincere." The girl bent her head, made for the door and murmured: "I'll set the table."

The signora went after her and repeated: "You have not been sincere."

Ida started spreading out the table-cloth, drew out the edges carefully, then muttered: "Perhaps you're right, signora, perhaps I haven't behaved well." She swallowed hastily and went on: "But you have your house, your family, and when I made you cross, you still had all that,

34

whereas I, as you know, I'm on my own."

"Yes," the signora said slowly, "that is true."

In Ida's little bedroom the wardrobe was open and on her bed were her big suitcase and her bag, already packed. Ida was busy folding up the last few garments. The house was silent, as it always was in the morning.

"Is everything ready?" asked the signora. "Are you leaving already?"

"What is there for me to do here?" replied Ida. "I've made my mind up now. I don't belong here any more, to this house, or to you."

The signora lowered her head and said quietly: "Of course, that's right. But to me it seems impossible that you're going away."

Ida looked at her: she was pale and her eyes dilated and seemed to grow larger. She said hastily: "Yes, it's bad for me too. I feel the same as when I leave Sardinia after my holiday, and I tell myself: Today I'm here and tomorrow I'll be in Rome, and I'm leaving my home and my people and I feel very bad." She contemplated the little room, the picture postcards stuck on the gilt drawing-pins and sat down on the bed. The signora took her by the arm, held it hard and murmured, "Good luck," but tears started down her cheeks and her voice failed her.

"What are you doing? What on earth are you doing?"

The signora looked at her for a moment with sorrow, affection, anger: "Go," she whispered, "you'd better go."

She stood in the kitchen drying her tears. She propped herself against the table and after a while heard to her relief the front door shutting. She thought of Ida's bent figure with that great suitcase. She felt a profound grief and was glad to be alone in the house, but was unable to calm herself. Her mind went over so many things, she had a pain in the heart, and she went on drying her tears, when a picture

35

came to mind of herself as a little girl at her uncle's house in the country, going down with the women into the kitchen garden to draw water from the well. The women would lift up the heavy iron cover and she, standing on tip-toes, would peer curiously inside the well, and first she would see darkness and then her eyes would make out the water-line and the light glinting off the surface and the midges sitting on the water and then, looking down deeper, she would divine a zone of green shadow and then black shadow and below that she still peered and peered but could not see down to the very bottom of the well.

She laid her hand on her heart, looked inside herself and strove to understand, then she felt that somehow she had failed in her quest.

Playing games

Angelica gazed from her corner, entranced, at the garden; at the mystery-gold light that touched the flower beds and deepened beneath the trees and along the surrounding wall. The garden was deserted. The little girl raced across it to the bed of geraniums that was in full sunshine. She stood beside the boxwood hedge, felt the warmth upon her hair and the intermittent buzz of insects. She scanned the villa's upper floor and for an instant she thought she saw the curtain at one of the windows quiver. She waited a few minutes, contemplated the intense red of the geraniums and plucked a few petals: then joyfully put them to her lips.

"My mouth is red," she thought, and gave a pleased smile.

She entered the villa, taking care not to make any noise. At once from the end of the hall her cousin appeared, looking anxious. She gazed hard at her, made a little grimace and whispered: "You've put petals on your lips." She added eagerly: "Shall we play? Well, then, shall we play?"

Angelica did not answer, but followed her. From the kitchen came a clink of crockery, otherwise there was silence throughout the villa. The two girls entered the sitting-room, where they were permitted to stay as they would not disturb the adults' afternoon nap.

"Are your parents already asleep?" asked Angelica.

Elvina's face darkened and she replied shrilly: "You know they're asleep. They sleep every afternoon."

Angelica raised her shoulders slightly and asked: "What about you? Why don't you sleep when they do?"

Elvina quickly replied: "I want to play with you." She hesitated a moment and added, "And besides, they don't want me with them." She pouted, and looked towards the ground.

The sitting-room shutters were closed but narrow shafts

37

of light came through and the multi-coloured bronze peacock that adorned the marble centre-piece on the table, caught by the sunlight, looked lovelier than ever. Angelica touched it and said complaisantly: "We'll play, if you like. But we'll play right over here, next to the table."

Elvina at once opened the straw basket she had brought with her.

"What would you like?" she asked. "Would you like the flowers, the feathers?"

Angelica looked into the little basket, brushed aside the feathers and began searching through the buttons.

"D'you see what a lot I've got?" prattled Elvina proudly. "Sometimes granny gives me some, too."

The door opened noiselessly and the house-maid thrust her head into the room. She said in an undertone: "Mind, children." And she put her finger to her lips. She regarded them suspiciously for a moment and went on: "What are you doing? Are you playing?" She gave a swift look round and shut the door without awaiting a reply.

Of the buttons, Angelica had chosen the ones like diamonds: some were loose, others were strung on a silk lilac ribbon. She said: "Let's pretend we're in a palace and put diamonds here and there, where they look best."

She looked around and adorned the furniture and objects which she found shabby with her shining little buttons. Elvina followed her approvingly: "Shall I put some flowers out too?" she asked. And, imitating her cousin, she laid her little posies of artificial flowers on the arm-rests and window-sills.

When the room was ready, Angelica smiled happily and reflected that it had become most beautiful, just the place for her game.

"And now?" asked Elvina. "What now?"

Angelica slowly seated herself on the hide armchair and crossed her legs. She loved the cool feel of the leather against her bare legs. And she loved those brief instants of expectancy when Elvina gazed at her and everything was as she desired it to be.

A slight shuffling sound came from the floor above, then a soft thud as of something falling, and some unsteady foot-falls on the floor.

Angelica looked upwards and thought: granny's getting

up already. She glanced at her cousin and murmured: "Granny was in a bad mood, don't you think?"

"Didn't she speak?" asked Elvina.

"Not a word," said Angelica, "right through lunch."

"Let's play," resumed Elvina. "Come on, let's play."

But Angelica's mind was elsewhere. She thought, I wonder whether she'll speak tonight. She said gracelessly: "But do I always have to take the lead?"

Elvina looked at her, annoyance and anger flashing in her great dark eyes. She cried: "Aren't you here to play with me?"

Angelica looked at her cousin and retorted: "And if I weren't here, what would you do?" She reddened and, with trembling voice, went on: "Without me, you're bored. And you copy me. You always copy me."

Elvina shook her head vigorously and cried: "It's not true. You're making things up." She raised her hand to strike her playmate, but restrained herself. She went and sat on the divan, looked the other way and muttered: "I can play on my own, you'll see."

The telephone could be heard ringing some way off and straight after, the footsteps of the house-maid crossing the hallway. "Uncle and Aunty must have woken up at last," thought Angelica. And she sat listening out for the noises of the household. The rays of sunshine were slanting more obliquely into the room: here and there the tiny diamond buttons gleamed like little lights and the peacock with his fine blues and golds and oranges was ablaze on the table centre. Angelica, gazing at these things, smiled and thought: how lovely they look. She brightened up again and said: "We'll play, if you like." She rose to her feet and whispered: "I'll start, all right?"

She picked up a little oval enamelled metal box, opened it slowly and held the two halves in her hand a good while.

"What are you doing?" asked Elvina in a low voice, as if under a spell. She hadn't moved from her place and kept asking: "What are you going to do?"

Angelica gazed at the two parts of the box, undid the buttons of her blouse and slid the two halves under her vest, one on either side of her chest. She thrust out her chest, drew her blouse tight at the waist with her hands and, with hot cheeks and heaving heart, whispered: "How do I look, Elvina?"

39

They looked at each other breathlessly. The house was in deep silence once more. Elvina broke into a strange laugh, her eyes looked paler, greyish, her face became serious again, she stretched out a hand and murmured: "May I try too?"

The cousins tip-toed past their grandmother's room, held their breath as they ran up the stairs and entered the low-ceilinged room where they were not allowed to play.

Elvina clapped her hands and cried: "They haven't heard us." She flung herself on the single bed covered with a white cotton coverlet and said: "Just imagine if they'd noticed."

Angelica slowly shut the solid door and replied: "Don't shout." She too was excited. She crossed the attic and stood where the ceiling was lowest and she could almost touch it if she raised her arm. She said: "I've grown, don't you think?"

Elvina raised her shoulders and replied: "I'm almost as big as you are."

Angelica abruptly lowered her arm and asked: "Why don't your parents want us to come here?"

Elvina started clutching at the hair that was hanging down over her eyes and answered unwillingly: "Because it's the guest room. Granny says it's always got to be kept tidy."

Angelica immediately thought: but what if no one ever comes. Then she recalled a distant cousin of her aunts, a sea-captain who a long time ago had turned up unexpectedly and had stayed a few days at the villa. In the evenings he told long stories about his travels, but interrupted himself from time to time to pay compliments to her aunts: he'd look at them with a smile and a half-bow and seemed to be hinting at something which only they could grasp. They laughed a lot. Angelica reddened and kept repeating to herself, what a stupid man. Really stupid.

Elvina, who was studying her expression, asked point-blank: "What are you thinking about?"

Angelica gestured vaguely: so many thoughts were going through her head, but she did not care to share them with anybody, and she did not reply.

Elvina tried another tack, and asked: "What will you do when you're grown up, Angelica?"

Her cousin retorted quickly: "What will you do? You tell me first."

Elvina bit her lip, cast an anxious glance at her cousin and said: "I don't know. I don't know."

Angelica paid no more attention to her. She gazed at the dormer window through which a bright light streamed into the room that was very different from that in the ordinary rooms, and at the water-colours painted by her uncle who had died in the war: a wood with sunshine glinting through the trees and a meadow full of flowers. She especially loved that wood, the pale yellow glow between the slender tree trunks. As she looked at it she could hear her aunts reminiscing about their own childhood with changed voices and eyes, while she herself roamed with them through an era when she had not yet been born and felt as if she was wandering through a strange land. She nearly always ended by thinking of that uncle who had died so young: and the strange thought that slowly came over her pushed her along towards other mysterious and unexplored regions.

A swallow darted close past the dormer and its shadow appeared fleetingly large.

Elvina was still sitting on the bed, weaving her fingers along the curlicues of the coverlet. Angelica drew near to her and said quietly: "We could come here every afternoon."

Elvina looked startled and replied: "You know Granny is against it."

"But if she doesn't know."

Elvina gave a flicker of a smile and said: "That's true. She hasn't heard us today." She reflected a while, gave her cousin a searching look and asked: "But what shall we do here?"

Angelica also came and sat on the bed, looked towards the dormer window, which at that moment framed a sky full of white clouds, and said distantly: "Nothing. But I still like it."

Angelica and Elvina were in the play-room of the two sisters Anna and Maria. Anna put aside some comics, went and stood in front of the mirror and asked listlessly: "What d'you want to play?"

They looked at each other. Angelica lowered her gaze because she was shy and these older girls were daughters of a friend of her uncle and aunt's and she'd met them only a few times.

Maria said: "A pity it's raining, or we could go and run around in the garden."

Maria was a tall, tubby girl. When she spoke, saliva gathered at the corners of her mouth, which Angelica found very ugly. But she recognized that Maria was a nice girl. They dawdled around the room. Anna, the younger sister, caught Maria by the arm and said in an undertone: "Let's act. What do you say?"

"Yes," said Angelica at once. "Yes, I'd like that." And she gave Elvina a look which said: you'd better like it, too. She looked at her reflection in the window-pane, which showed her small blond head and high cheek-bones. She smiled at herself and repeated: I do like acting. At school the teacher always chooses me. She suddenly fell silent, feeling shy of talking about herself. She would have liked to express her pleasure more aptly, but joy, like any emotion, made her self-conscious.

Anna laughed, and cried out: "Come on, let's prepare a scene."

Elvina gave the two sisters a perplexed look and asked: "What will I have to do?"

Anna looked at her friend, who was the youngest of all of them, and said: "You're the youngest. You can be the chambermaid."

She took an embroidered handkerchief out of a drawer and, tying it on around her hair, added with a laugh: "Here's your cap."

Elvina gave a bow, and then another, then thought: I wonder what they'll make me do? This worried her.

Maria clapped her hands and said: "Come here. I'll tell you. Once we pretended a stranger had come from afar and then it was discovered that he came from the world of the dead." And as she recalled it, her eyes darkened.

Angelica's heart began to pound, she looked at the elder

girl and asked timidly: "But where will we act?"

The sisters exchanged glances and Maria said: "This room's the theatre, isn't that right, Anna? Now I'll shut the window and turn on the light. I'll dress you up as a ghost."

They were all highly excited, but Angelica was the most worked up. Anna had opened the wardrobe and was fishing out hats, a fan and some oddments of brightly coloured cloth. She put on a man's hat and laughed. Then she picked up a long white veil and murmured: "Here, Angelica, this is for you." She went up to her and fixed the veil on her so as to cover her head.

The room was almost in darkness. Maria had closed the shutters. A small, shaded lamp had been placed on the floor in one corner. Anna shifted the table and chairs. She went up to her sister and they mumbled together, chuckling from time to time.

"What are you saying?" asked Elvina. "I want to know, too."

Then Maria left her sister, picked up a stool, planted it in the middle of the room and ordered: "Angelica, stand on top of this. Stand still. All you've got to do is stand still."

Angelica climbed on to the stool and felt as tall as if her head reached into the clouds.

Elvina whispered: "What about me? Where shall I go?"

"Silence," said Maria. "I'll direct you later."

The two sisters could again be heard mumbling together and Elvina was saying: Anna, give me your hand.

Angelica made an effort to keep still. The veil that came down over her face made her hot and she felt she wasn't breathing properly. She looked at her arms and noticed that they were a dead white, quite different from usual. Her joy had completely evaporated. She waited for something to happen and in that silence broken by rustlings and mumblings she felt a tightness at her chest and a great unhappiness.

She heard a little girl sobbing aloud. A commotion ensued and Anna cried out: "Lights. Turn on the light."

As soon as the light was on, Maria said: "Angelica, why are you crying? Why are you crying?" She made her get off the stool at once and gave her a hug. "The poor dear," she mumbled to her sister. "She's had a fright."

Anna nodded and sighed. But she burst out laughing and said: "What can she be frightened of? It's only us here."

Angelica was still clinging to Maria because that large warm body comforted her greatly. Elvina was still in her corner and was partly relieved and partly annoyed that the game had been interrupted. She stared at her cousin in amazement because she'd behaved in such an unusual manner, she wanted to ask her for some kind of explanation but didn't know quite what.

Angelica couldn't believe it was actually her that had been crying. She let go of Maria's hand and said: "It wasn't me crying."

Anna glanced at her sister and a sly look flashed in her eyes. Maria muttered: "Don't," and whispered something in her ear.

Angelica was glad that none of the girls were paying her any attention, because she didn't want to talk about what had happened.

Maria went and opened the shutters. The weather had turned fine again and from the open window could be seen the lofty canopies of the lime trees. The rain had made their scent stronger and some of it wafted into the room.

Anna went to the mirror and started combing her curly hair that had got ruffled during their game. Her cheeks were red and her eyes alert. She said: "I've enjoyed myself quite a bit, though."

In a corner by the wardrobe lay the coloured hats and stuff.

Now Angelica had calmed down. But she was still left in a slight wonderment and dread. Right through that summer and beyond she recollected that afternoon with keen regret at having spoiled such a splendid game. And she mused in bewilderment: but how could I have given myself such a scare?

Rehearsals

Carlo went out into the garden, the row of ancient, great plane trees ran down one side, throwing their shade upon the gravel. Here and there beside the flower-beds stood elegant, capacious wicker armchairs for the guests, beyond the hedge was the azure haze of the sea.

"Good morning," a light voice said. "Good morning."

Carlo turned round and saw in the large armchair, almost lost in it, a slight figure, its face in shadow, its eyes dark and meek.

He stopped, and said: "Good morning, Alda. You're staying here, too?"

Alda replied: "I was very tired, I needed to rest. We moved to Rome at the end of the school year."

"Are you pleased?"

Alda shrugged, and said: "I don't know." She reflected for a moment, smiled at herself and added: "I'm curious and scared at one and the same time, and sô I go on."

Carlo looked at her: "Come to the theatre some time, if that might please you. We're rehearsing. What about your husband?"

"He's taken our son to his grandmother's. He'll be involved in the Congress here in a few days from now."

The three of them were sitting at some distance from one another as after all they weren't friends, but guests at the same hotel enjoying civil fellowship.

Signora Pieri glanced at the sky, at the first fallen shrivelled leaves, and said: "You see, signora Alda? My son has arrived."

Alda smiled and replied: "I recognized him at once. We met last year."

There was a silence. Carlo fetched out his pipe and tobacco pouch. Signora Pieri resumed: "I was pleased to see him. But he's come to tell us he wants to drop his course. It's the second time he's changed his mind. These things are worrying, dear God. It makes you wonder: is he so unsettled? My husband is becoming very bad-tempered and keeps saying he won't do this and he won't do that and I sometimes wait till he's let off steam and then I say: be quiet, just think, he's alive, at least he's alive."

Signora Pieri's eyes as she said this had grown very large and her pale green irises were full of anxiety and love.

Alda looked at her, while a shudder ran through her: she was thinking of her own lovely little boy and all of a sudden the years ahead appeared in an unknown guise. She passed a hand across her forehead and said slowly: "Everything's so difficult, and then for young people. I think one needs a lot of patience."

"Yes," said signora Pieri, "but it's no simple matter. It isn't, believe me."

Carlo began poking away at his pipe and said: "I have no children, but I do have some idea."

Alda glanced at him and could not work out whether those words contained some regret, but Carlo went on: "And I wonder whether anyone can really help a young man make his choices."

He rose and nodded a greeting at the two ladies: "I really must be off. The rehearsal's already begun."

Signora Pieri also stood up: she was somewhat short and stout, but had a mobile and sensitive face. She put one hand on her chest and seemed to let the words escape her: "My God, will everything work out all right? What do you say, signora Alda, will everything work out all right?"

Alda was flustered, she would have liked to find something reassuring to say, but all she could come out with was: "But of course, what can you be thinking of? Everything will turn out all right."

Alda entered the almost empty and almost dark theatre, tip-toed across the aditorium and sat down beside Carlo.

On the stage the actors were rehearsing wearily. The sound of hammering could be heard from backstage and two workmen were hoisting vertically upwards along the sides of the stage the framework of two series of white windows that were to be the wings.

"What d'you think of them?" asked Carlo in a low voice. "Mind you, the producer is making new demands now, he's changing his approach."

Alda nodded. She recalled a street she had to follow on her way to school as a little girl, those old buildings had just that type of window. She smiled in the dark and said: "I like them. They've got atmosphere."

"In spite of which, I'm going to have to get rid of them." Carlo gestured his dismay and added: "The director is calling for other props, and the stage would get too cluttered."

"Pity," said Alda, and looked again at the windows dangling in mid-air.

The costume designer approached Carlo and in an undertone requested some guidance from him. Carlo got up and followed him.

The director was sitting in one of the front rows and seemed engrossed in thought. Nearby, at a lamp-lit table, sat the assistant director. On the stage, the young actress appeared. She was wearing blue-jeans and a nineteenth-century style lace blouse. She'd pulled her hair up over her forehead, possibly to help her get into her part. Her pale blue eyes shone and twinkled agreeably. At her entrance the lead actor livened up again and they began their scene intensely.

The girl recited: "If you always spoke to me like that, tenderly, gently, how easy our life would be. I ask nothing of you. But you can't stop me from dreaming of a different life, with the two of us together, but really together."

Alda settled back in her seat: an understanding had been born between the two actors and their words floated on the air at once strong and light. Carlo came back to his seat and after a while she whispered to him: "This is good. I like it."

Carlo concurred and seemed attentive and relaxed.

Across the narrow space between them and the actors the dialogue rang out, the emotions pulsed, yet none of it was real.

Signora Olga, in her deck chair, was holding her head erect and contemplating the sea. Her white-streaked hair was done up in a little chignon that showed up to advantage the hairline of her nape and forehead.

Alda was lying on the sand beside her, propping herself up on her elbows so as to keep her head up. She could see the rectangular shadows of the beach huts, snippets of intense blue sky and, out of the corner of her eyes, whenever she turned slightly, the beach, white in the sun's glare. Occasionally a child would run down to the sea, late bathers strolled along the sand at the water's edge and left footprints which were soon washed out.

Carlo and his wife walked by. They were talking away, both tall, spare figures. Signora Olga remarked: "Mara's arrived."

Alda followed them with her eyes and nodded, then asked: "Do you know them well, signora?"

Olga smiled and said: "Oh, yes. Carlo was a friend of my sons. They played together as children. They lived near us. At that time opposite our houses were meadows, sheep, wonderful for the children. It seems like another world, doesn't it?"

"Have Carlo and Mara been married long?"

The signora seemed preoccupied, she shook her head and said: "There were a lot of difficulties in their way, Carlo was married and, to be with him, Mara . . . ."

"They are very close, aren't they?"

Olga pursed her lips, looked into the distance, then said: "Very much so, very much so."

Alda played with the sand, stood up, squatted down again close to the signora's *chaise-longue* and murmured: "Yet so many years have gone by, over twenty, I believe?"

Signora Olga glanced at the other woman, lowered her head and said in a low voice, smiling to herself: "But the years don't count."

Alda blushed, her shy eyes grew larger. She said: "Oh God, I thought they did, at times. Isn't that how it is?"

Signora Olga shook her head, a flicker crossed her ravaged face and she said: "No, that isn't how it is. For me, it's always like the first time."

There was a moment's silence, and a quiet wave of emotion moved between the two women.

Mara and Carlo appeared coming round the beach hut.

"How are you?" Mara asked Alda. "I think we've met?"

Alda reddened and said: yes, yes. She could think of nothing else to say and signora Olga, Mara and Carlo began to talk of other things. Mara kept laughing, her voice sounded husky, at times almost dark, as her eyes were, at times.

She began describing her journey.

"Our *rapido* was stopped shortly after departure," she said. "There had been a rumour that someone had planted a bomb on the train."

Signora Olga was alarmed, kept shaking her little head and saying: "You can't live your life any more, can you conceive of it? Were you very frightened?"

Mara shrugged and replied: "Only for a minute. We threw ourselves down on the embankment. Some passengers said that an agitated fellow in a dark red shirt had appeared in their compartment. He'd set off the alarm bell and almost immediately jumped out of the train, a railwayman gave chase to him but the man, waving a pistol, shouted: I've planted a bomb on the train, I'll shoot. The railwayman hesitated and the man disappeared into the fields. Then we waited for the police and the explosives experts; everyone was talking at once, everyone was highly excited, there was just one old man who'd collapsed on the grass verge and was still trembling."

Signora Olga asked at once: "Was it really a madman?"

"Yes," said Carlo. "It seems he really was." He looked at the ground and added in an undertone: "But does it really make much difference?"

"What horrible going-on," went on signora Olga, in a changed voice. "I live in perpetual anxiety, I'm always thinking of my children and my husband."

She held out her hand to Carlo, who helped her to her feet. Alda also stood up. A soft breeze came from the sea, the women lifted up their faces as if the better to savour that moment, and the wind ruffled their hair.

Signora Olga gave her friends an affectionate look and said: "We'll be keeping each other company, won't we?"

Mara replied: "Of course we will. But first I'm going to have a bathe."

Carlo said: "Alda, will you dine with us?"

Alda replied hurriedly: "No, no. I've got to go up to my room, I've got to make some phone-calls."

Alda went up to her room. The receptionist had handed her a postcard from her little boy and his grandmother. She looked at it, turned it round in her hands and thought: his handwriting's nice, it seems older.

She started undressing slowly, hung up her dress on a hanger, set the shutters ajar so as to moderate the glare that was still powerful, picked up her book and took a seat. Immediately, she could see Carlo. It was a peaceful afternoon, there was silence, footsteps on the gravel from time to time or the sound of a distant scooter. She thought of the theatre, the actors' gestures, Carlo's presence, and again she felt she was entering that circle of light.

They were rehearsing the scene between the girls and their parents. Youthfulness and the randomness of emotion were the keynote of the scene and the girls, with their fresh faces and their colourful wide skirts, conveyed it well enough. The actor moved maladroitly from one of the girls to the other, as his role required. He held out his arm towards the prettiest and acted earnestly: "Don't run off. Let me speak. I love you. May I tell your father?" And the girl retorted: "I can't imagine how you dreamt up such an idea. You're joking, as usual." The skirmish continued lively and amusing. One of the sisters, barely in her 'teens, took the limelight and recited clearly: "I might marry you, if I were to consider taking a husband. However, I want to be a writer, that's all I dream of." The little girl of the family ran across the stage, sowing havoc. Life's humours, magnetic fields of attraction and repulsion, minds calculating or reckless, many delusions could be sensed at work.

The director called out: "Faster. Stop. Sorry. Speed up, it's almost got to be like a ballet."

There was a confabulation, the actors returned to their starting-points, there was some throat-clearing. The lead actor started off again with the line: don't run off, let me speak. The tempo quickened, but almost every effort sounded mechanical, the charmed moment of inspiration had slipped away.

Carlo watched in disappointment: a heart-wringing yearning for youth had stolen into him.

They halted on the terrace of the Palace. The sun was setting behind them, the beach had already been invaded by shadow and the sea was grey-blue and puckered. Carlo turned to look at Alda: she quivered and reddened over nothing at all, just because she liked or didn't like something or because someone noticed her. She was breathing a little faster. Carlo turned pale and gave a start. Alda asked: "What's the matter?"

Carlo smiled at himself and muttered: "Nothing, I was just thinking." He altered his tone and asked: "Will you be coming to the rehearsals?"

Alda nodded and said: "Your play is very good, are you pleased?"

"Oh, forget that." Carlo cocked his head to one side as he often did and began to speak rapidly. "One afternoon last spring while I was going to the theatre by taxi we ran into a demonstration. The driver, cursing away, took another route, but two or three times over we ran up against packs of youths who were yelling and rushing this way and that, running amok, and I was almost afraid. I can still see myself that afternoon witnessing the scenes of aggression in the town, my arrival at the theatre almost sheepish, the actor's taped voice and the fantastic golden light of the set." He lowered his voice, which was distinct and precise, and added: "I think we're all schizophrenic."

Alda asked: "But what about your painting? You never mention it."

Carlo's face clouded over and he interrupted her: "It's too difficult to talk about art. For the time being I'm painting stage scenery."

The sun had set. A big roller curled up the beach and its strong salt tang reached them. They left the terrace and went on walking. They were overtaken by a girl in oriental trousers closed in at the ankles and adorned with little silver bells that tinkled at her every movement. Alda and Carlo were drawn to look at her: but her gait was uneven, from time to time she'd lift up her arms or her face and address the air. She ran across the street and walked on along the opposite pavement, still lifting up her face or her arm and several passers-by turned round to look at her. Alda and Carlo could no longer hear her tinkling bells, but could make out her little figure, which looked at once cheerful and sinister.

Alda took a seat a little more than halfway up the auditorium, that seemed to her the best distance. She also enjoyed watching the performance from the stage because she felt she was getting deeper into the scene.

The actor recited: "My mind was engaged with other images, far-off emotions. I could see myself as a child, still in petticoats, when I would look up and ask: am I good or wicked?"

The assistant director showed a passage of the script to the director and the latter got up, went up to the footlights and said: "Sorry, my dear fellow: I'd like to see more of you. Take a couple of steps forward and lift your face up."

The actor said: all right, but he was out of humour. He took a couple of steps forward and mumbled the line again, throwing it away.

The assistant went over to Carlo swiftly and whispered: here we go.

From above came a brief command, almost at once the spotlights positioned over the first row of seats came on. The space expanded in a great sweep, the set, which up to then had seemed limp, livened up, things lost their heaviness and the actors seemed to move more smoothly, like fishes in water. The lighting changed, a spotlight followed the lead actor up to the front of the stage, picking him out, and showed up the hard-set, closed mask of his face.

Carlo got up, did a half turn, turned towards Alda again

and through his eyes shot a gleam of pleasure and as she watched him, she thought he suddenly looked younger. Carlo made a sweeping gesture with his hand and murmured: "There you are, that's theatre."

They met a little way from the hotel. Alda, when she saw them, quickened her pace and joined Carlo and Mara. The colour of approaching evening made their faces look dark, almost earthen. Alda felt something, an awkwardness perhaps, but thought it was her shyness, thrust aside any other idea and asked: "How did the rehearsals go today?"

Carlo seemed to reflect, touched his forehead and said: "There are some good moments, other situations haven't been resolved."

"Perhaps they will be."

Carlo stopped, cocked his head on one side and answered: "I don't think so. In the theatre it's difficult to leap up a level." The two women had stopped, too. Mara darkened and said: "Bah, theatre: I lived it once, now I can't bear it."

Alda looked at her in surprise and asked: "But don't you follow Carlo?"

"Yes, yes," answered Mara, "when I can. I also have my own commitments."

They walked on. Night was falling and clouds were massing to seaward. Alda cleared her throat and said uncertainly: "I've enjoyed following the rehearsals."

"Why?" asked Mara. "May I ask why?"

"I don't know," said Alda quietly, "I feel I've learnt things, rhythms."

"Poppycock," laughed Mara loudly, "utter poppycock."

They passed by the Belvedere, over the horizon the sky was violet-black, and as he contemplated it, Carlo was reminded of his mother's portrait. It was a fine painting done in the Twenties by a painter friend of his parents, and it showed his mother's face as fragile, sensitive and tender. He mused: I love the picture of my mother more than I do my mother. He banished that thought, he banished the images of childhood which were lying in wait for him, then sensed a void: more than that, he sensed a great distance and also a

furious vexation. He made two or three mechanical gestures and looked like a puppet whose strings are being slack-
ened. Alda felt ill at ease, wanted to break the silence, turn
to Mara but saw her distant and impatient look and lost the
desire to speak. She thought: maybe I'd better have gone to
the mountains with the child. She said: "Shall we walk
faster? I'm almost cold."

They walked quickly to the hotel. It was dark, there were
few people about, a bicycle without lights brushed past
Alda, who started in alarm. Carlo looked at her with indif-
ference and said nothing.

The actors had shut themselves away in a changing room
for a union meeting. The director was talking about it in
hushed tones to the theatre manager, the stage hands carried
on working and there was a peaceful babble behind the
scenes, two lads were busy coating the furniture with a
special grey-blue and the electricians were calling out to
each other from one part of the theatre to the other.

Carlo descended into the auditorium. He took a seat near
the back and sat there taking in his stage setting, mentally
inserting and removing passages. At centre stage a white
sheet had been lowered over the furniture, to be slowly
raised a few minutes before the start of the performance. It
was a great shapeless mass. Carlo stared at it, the air seemed
to be laced with something of the life of the play, of the
author, of the actors and even of what was going on outside,
in the distance, the violence. He recalled to mind an old
painting of his and realized he had tried to convey by it that
same quality of emotion and anguish. He closed his eyes.
The assistant called him: Carlo? Carlo?

When he spotted him, he went up to him and said:
"They're raising the sheet soon. Keep your eyes open." He
smiled and remarked: "It's underneath it that memories lie,
that's to say, life."

Carlo made a nervous gesture, tilted his head and muttered through gritted teeth: "For goodness' sake. Let's just
see how it works."

"You're so pale. Are you all right?"

"I've got my usual headache," answered Carlo.

In the side doorway stood Mara, her large eyes upon him, looking as if she'd been there for all eternity. Carlo got up and went over to join her. On the stage the sheet, hoisted from above, began to rise, its off-white mass palpitating.

"I like walking along the shore," said Mara, "I walk for kilometres at a time." She paused and then asked: "Do you want to come with me?"

Alda looked doubtfully at her but said: "Yes, I'll come."

They walked along the line between sand and sea, they were surrounded by voices and cries of children which were immediately carried away by the wind, they often looked out towards the boundless sea.

"I've been as far as the end of the beach," said Mara. "You know? Where the rocks begin."

"Yes," answered Alda, "I know the place, I've been coming here for so many years."

Mara started talking. "Yesterday was a strange evening. I remembered there was going to be a broadcast in which I'd taken part, but at the last minute I discovered that there's no television in the hotel. I ran out to the nearest bar, which was closed, so I walked quite a long way through the night. I came at last into a place which was open to find that the programme had already begun, while people at the table close by were playing cards and the girl behind the bar was glancing vacantly at the screen; and all at once I realized I wasn't interested in the broadcast either. As she spoke, she waved her hands about, her eyes were intense and she said again: "Do you understand?" There, at that particular moment, I asked myself what *did* really matter to me. And I wasn't able to give an answer or perhaps there is no answer."

They had stopped and were eyeing each other while the wave sucked away at the sand from under their feet. Alda would have liked to say: but you have an interesting job, however she immediately thought that wouldn't be the right remark and so she said: "I do understand, you know. There are moments, some moments." She groped for words.

Mara's eyes seemed to turn more sombre. She nodded two or three times, then glanced at Alda, who was gazing at her, altered her expression and spoke again lightly: "When I got back to the hotel I was very depressed, then Carlo arrived and I calmed down. Carlo has this power over me."

Alda thought: how emotional she is. She also thought she was lying as regards Carlo and couldn't explain to herself why she felt a growing anxiety and mistrust. She took a hasty breath and said: "Shall we go back?"

They retraced their steps. The wind caressed their bodies and filled out the white sails upon the sea.

The actor was rehearsing his monologue. Some of the cast descended into the auditorium to follow it better. Carlo and Alda were sitting in the centre box.

The assistant director came in and asked in a whisper: "Do you like that overcoat on him?"

Carlo nodded.

The assistant director sat down behind them and said quietly: "I think he's very good."

The musical and sound effects were also being tried out. A dull, long-drawn-out booming of cannon occasionally became audible as a background to the monologue. The actor came slowly forward to the front of the stage, face up-turned, and his painful expression was striking. The stage was luridly lit.

Mara entered the auditorium by the side door. She glanced round rapidly, saw Carlo and Alda in the box, but sat down in one of the front rows. The actor was reciting: "Perhaps the malady that caused me those mysterious pains is simply life. It's no trifling malady, in fact it's always mortal. Any attempt at progress is just a delusion."

The director raised his arm to interrupt the speech. Mara also waved a greeting to the actor. The latter came up to the footlights and shouted: "The background noise is disturbing my concentration. It's upsetting me a great deal, d'you understand or don't you?"

He paced up and down on the stage for a moment, spotted Mara and asked her at once: "Did you hear my monologue?"

Mara replied: "No, I've only just arrived."

She sprang to her feet and dashed out. The door, flung open wide, went on swinging a good while. The director waited for the tension to subside, then said to the actor: "Shall we continue?"

Carlo had turned a vivid red. He arched his eyebrows and sat still, staring at centre stage. After a few minutes he said: "I'm off. I've finished for today."

Alda stayed in her seat. The actor was continuing his monologue. He recited it with gravity, Alda listened to it feelingly and her heart felt tight and anxious.

When the actor had ended, his words seemed to die out in a silence that was thronged with echoes. The actors in the auditorium clapped their hands in token applause, the director stood up and said loudly: "Good, very good."

The actor rubbed a hand over his eyes, relaxed and said: "I can do better. Today something's been distracting me."

The director smiled and repeated: "No, no, I swear to you, you were very good."

A young colleague had climbed on to the stage and was embracing the lead actor, the two whispered together and walked off arm in arm into the wings. The director slowly went after them.

The assistant director picked up the script, stretched out his arms with a sigh and headed for the exit, the stage mechanics walked across the stage talking loudly, then their voices faded away. The stage was still lit as if by the warm glow of a fire. Alda, standing in her box, pressed her fingers hard into the plush, felt that there were things there, but that they couldn't be grasped.

Little lamps with shades had been lit in the garden on the tables laid for dinner. The waitresses moved swiftly from table to table. Some of the gests were already seated, others were still arriving and going to their seats.

Alda went to her table and nodded a greeting to Carlo who was already eating. A lampstand cast its light upon the lower branches of the birch-tree in the middle, making the light leaves transparent and bright, the border of zinnias, by contrast, lacking direct light, appeared violet-coloured, almost black.

The maître-d'hotel came up to Alda and asked her: "Has your husband arrived?"

"No," said Alda, "he'll be here tomorrow at the earliest."

They brought her the hors-d'oeuvre and she started eating listlessly. A strong smell of grilled meat which upset her had filled the air. She had a look round, the guests were busy with their food, the maître-d'hotel was giving advice and taking down orders. She looked at Carlo and thought his face was still a little drawn and there seemed to be something elusive in his vivid eyes. She took her mind off him: in front of her, in her favourite corner, sat the glorious old actress who always ended her holiday in that hotel every year. Her hair was snow-white, her painted mouth had a bitter twist and whenever she spoke, even in a low voice, her words were resonant. Alda contemplated her, her curiosity aroused, and she too felt very much alone. She finished her meal quickly and went up to her room.

When Carlo saw that Alda had disappeared, he remained a long time deep in thought. He left his table and walked across the garden, not looking at anyone, with quick, nervous strides. He had to go to the theatre for a rehearsal, but he decided to take a long way round. He had a headache and was oppressed by conflicting emotions.

He reached the Belvedere, it had started blowing a little and he was struck by the sound of the undertow, the sea could hardly be seen because it was a starless night. That great blackness overwhelmed him.

Two workmen were measuring out the garden boundaries. A little girl, a few steps away from them, watched their comings and goings with intense curiosity and with graceful little gestures, but the moment they addressed her, she would run off to hide behind a tree. Alda followed her game.

A ship sounded its hooter far away, then the hooter sounded again, more briefly and at regular intervals.

Mara went across the garden, disappeared, reappeared.

Someone called to the little girl sternly: *Claire, viens, viens.* The girl stiffened on her little legs and shook her head as if to drive away a tiresome thought.

A pale sun gleamed upon the garden. The first Congress participants had arrived, they were standing outside the entrance, talking loudly.

Again came the foreign voice calling: *Claire, Claire.* The old actress stopped for an instant beside the child, then moved on without a smile.

Mara recrossed the garden, caught sight of Alda and looked away. She changed her mind and went up to her.

Alda partly rose from her chair, she was about to speak but Mara interrupted her and said: "Carlo's gone."

Alda gestured her surprise. Her heart beat faster and she answered: "I didn't know. What about the rehearsals?"

"He'll be back in a couple of days, I think. He was called away on a job."

There was a silence, each of the two women was following her own train of thought and could not get out of it. Signora Olga was heard to ask gently, has my husband got back? Fragmented words and laughter drifted across from the Congress participants.

The little girl had gone up to the two men, she was looking at them with a smile and held out her hand to them.

Mara went on as if to herself: "Now everybody's after him. In the theatre all he has to do is choose."

Alda said: "Carlo is brilliant."

"You needn't tell me that," retorted Mara sharply. "I've always said so. But it's taken years."

She fell silent and a crease appeared between her eyebrows.

The little girl had squatted down on the flower-bed that skirted the boundary wall and was holding earth and stones in her hands: she was looking around with an air of mingled defiance and alarm. Mara followed Alda's gaze, cleared her throat and went on, seemingly calmer: "You have a child, haven't you?"

"Yes," said Alda. "He's with his grandmother in the mountains."

"Have you any problems?"

Alda was taken aback, smitten by a deep-seated uneasiness. She replied energetically: "Oh no. He's a lovely boy."

"I have plenty of friends with serious problems," said Mara. "They no longer know what to do, they aren't sure of anything. I'm glad I haven't any children." She gave one of her harsh-sounding laughs, but her eyes were steady, and she added: "But two don't make a family. They do not. It's just as I am telling you."

Alda tried to look Mara in the eye, but she was already looking away. She wanted to reply, but only said: "Ah, family."

The foreign child's mother had appeared: she was gripping her by the arm and dragging her back to the hotel, the child was dragging her feet and her eyes were swelling with tears, her mother too was angry and her face and gestures betrayed utter impatience. Alda couldn't help following the scene and once again her thoughts turned anxiously to her own son.

Mara stood in front of her, taut as a crossbow. She said in a low voice: "Have I upset you, perhaps?"

Alda answered quietly: "I've been thinking of so many things." The sky was almost white, the leaves began to rustle and a dank gust swept the garden. She shivered and added: "It will rain soon."

Mara looked around with her sombre eyes and murmured: "It doesn't bother me. I'm leaving, anyway."

Alda went up to her room and began writing to her son: "My dear boy, thank you for your lovely card . . . These days there's hardly anyone on the beach and long rows of beach huts are already shut up . . . Tomorrow Brigitte's leaving, too. She's the little French girl I told you about. So are lots of other people . . ."

She woke at dawn. The shutters let through just a weak light. She heard or thought she heard some commotion, someone crying. The things in her room seemed to float as if weightless. She closed her eyes and tried to sleep. In her half-slumber she had a kind of dream in which she saw herself as a little girl but with her adult face. This caused her great distress.

In the morning the news spread rapidly. There had been a

phone call to say that something serious had happened to Carlo. Late in the day it was heard that he had died, and his friends gathered that the circumstances were not straightforward. Nobody could come to terms with it, nobody could avoid talking about it and the bewilderment was great. Signora Olga clutched her armchair, waxen-faced. Alda shut herself up in her room and burst into tears. A hot stream ran down her face, her hands. So she remained, motionless, her head filled with images.

She wanted to go to the funeral. She and her husband drove to the small town where Carlo had been born. It was a non-religious funeral, his aged mother was not present, nor was his wife. Many friends and colleagues were there. There were downpours of rain and a blustery wind and the umbrellas danced madly against the murky sky. Many people were weeping and there was the feeling that a terrible wound had been inflicted.

Alda was plunged for days in deep sadness. Carlo was inside her and she could not let go of him. She wrote asking her mother to keep the boy with her because she did not feel like seeing him and looking after him.

Candle-wax figurines

That summer I was taken to the seaside by aunt Irene. We had a large apartment with a long corridor and a row of rooms on either side and a square-shaped kitchen full of sunlight at the end. From the kitchen window, if you leaned out, you could see the little harbour and the sea.

I'd been given a quiet, cosy room with two high mahogany frame beds, white cotton bedspreads and a marble washstand. To get into bed at night I had to scale the side of my bed and I enjoyed heaving myself up and gazing around from that height. Aunt Irene looked rather old to me, was of middle height and had a pale complexion and thin lips. But her slightly slanting hazel brown eyes were beautiful and gentle.

The first time I was taken to her house was at Christmas. Someone had left me at the door saying: in you go, in you go, give them a surprise. I'd taken a few steps with my heart in my mouth. The lights were on everywhere, the doors to all the rooms were open and my cousin Leda was at her upright baby grand, singing. Her fine contralto notes filled the house.

I was rooted to the spot, following her singing and watching her hands moving swiftly over the keyboard and her head swaying with the flow of the music.

The room gleamed with brass ornaments, the song conjured up the East, diamonds and pearls. Aunt Irene appeared in the doorway: seeing me, she clasped her hands together in amazement. Leda, too, made much of me. They took me in to greet uncle Marco who was sitting at his account book in his study. Uncle Marco immediately wanted me to see his Nativity crib. We went to the other end of the apartment as the crib was in the end room, a through room which nobody used. The shutters in this room were closed, the centre light was masked in blue and tiny lights gleamed here and there on the pasteboard mountains that rose against the far wall.

My uncle released my hand and ushered me up to the crib, and the adults looked at me and asked: d'you like it? Well, then, d'you like it? I stood there feeling slightly uncomfortable. It was the first time I had seen a crib from so close to. The pasteboard, at the points where it turned upwards, was discoloured, the baby Jesus at the mouth of the stable had livid cheeks and Saint Joseph and the Madonna looked too large beside him. So I preferred not to see them and gazed beyond, where, along the tracks I could see the figures of shepherds, flocks, dogs and a sparkling brook.

I think it was the end of the winter. I lived in town and was at primary school when we had the news that uncle Marco had died. I was not told the news directly. For a few days I saw my mother looking a little sad and almost dazed, her sisters turned up and kept giving her questioning glances and mumbling: your brother-in-law, so suddenly, just like that, how come? And they confabulated amongst themselves, cutting me out of the conversation. It was the housemaid who told me uncle Marco had died, but perhaps when she told me I already knew it.

On the other hand, my father himself gave me the news of my grandmother's death. I remember there was some commotion in the house, someone said to me: run along, quick, your father's waiting for you at the gate; and a pullover was thrust into my arms.

We were walking along a road where the countryside had already started. My father gave me his hand to hold and kept his head bowed. He said: "Six days ago your grandmother Bice died. She was a good and holy woman, everybody loved her, not only us children, and I'm sorry that you, the youngest of her grandchildren, never got to know her better."

He drew a handkerchief from his pocket and mopped at tears which had sprung from his eyes. I gazed at his altered face and didn't know what to say, not a word would come to my lips and I could not capture the image of my granny Bice. With an effort, I recalled her pale face among other faces around the long dining table.

My father took me back home before it was dark, and left me at the door with a sorrowful embrace. Not until much later did I understand, the idea of death was then still distant and mysterious, and adult grief made me feel embarrassed.

After uncle Marco's death, aunt Irene and Leda left their old apartment and moved into a more modest dwelling. When I was taken there for the summer, little clues hinted to me that something had changed, and though no one referred openly to money and other worries, it was as though I knew there were things on their mind. Their new situation caused me some anxiety from time to time, because I was fond of the two women and I wished to see them happy. Maybe the creeping doubt had come over me, tormentingly, that things could change and appear otherwise than I had come to know them.

Still, aunt Irene appeared calm, and she always behaved sweetly and smilingly towards me, only she would say mournfully from time to time: "My life is over. Now I'd like to see Leda happily settled."

Leda would toss her fine curly hair and cry: "You look after yourself instead. It's time you took care of your own self, relaxed a bit."

In fact my aunt busied herself all day long and followed the housemaid's every move, sighing and turning her eyes heavenwards.

In the evening, when she saw me to my bedroom, she would remain a while at the foot of my bed and I would beg her: "Tell me a story. Please, tell me a story."

My aunt would shy away, say she didn't know any, but I would persist: "Tell me a story about the war," I entreated. "A story of when you were a girl."

She often repeated things I'd already heard, she told me

about her husband, who had feigned madness so as to avoid going to war, he'd grown a great beard and roamed around town gesticulating and ranting.

"And did they take him to be mad?" I asked, alarmed. "Did they really take him to be mad?" And I was full of concern over what might happen.

Once she told me of when they had first seen an Italian aircraft fly over their little town. They were on the harbourside, all was dark because of the blackout, but the weather was mild and plenty of people were out for a stroll. Suddenly they had heard that noise, a noise new to their ears, and the excitement was general. They had stayed out there for a good long while, even complete strangers embraced each other, they scanned the sky and talked about what had happened, for it had been such a great moment.

As my aunt told her story, her eyes shone, her face was animated, and something of those far-off times and the days of her youth got through to me.

I recollect that about half way along the corridor in aunt Irene's apartment was a small wooden door of a different shape and colour from the others. One afternoon when Leda was keeping herself quietly to herself, she said: "I'm going up into the attic. Would you like to come with me, little one?"

We opened the little door, went up some wooden stairs and found ourselves in the attic. It was long and narrow but had plenty of light, there were potatoes laid out on mats on the floor and there were trunks along the walls. Leda opened their lids and started fishing out old clothes, skirts, shawls and an evening dress in green shot silk. She held it up, set it against her body, but said, looking at herself with dissatisfaction: "It's no good, it's right out of fashion now."

She closed the trunk and sat down. There was silence in the attic, and a good smell of dry timber. Leda just sat there, arms folded, and seemed to be looking out of the dormer window which gave a view of the pier and a stretch of sea.

I was eyeing her and suddenly asked, with beating heart: "Leda, what's become of Paolo?"

Leda looked at me in surprise. Her expression had hardened. And, though I knew I should not have, I repeated: "But what's become of him?"

Leda frowned and said loudly: "Paolo is a rascal. I don't see him any more, I don't want to see him."

She had turned red and was looking into the distance again. So we stayed, without saying any more. I recollected going for a walk with the two of them. We were crossing a pine wood just outside the little town, the sun was setting, its light filtered through the trees and we trod lightly over the slippery floor of pine needles. Paolo was asking me about school, about my life in town during the winter, and I, usually so shy, readily answered his questions and was pleased that this good-looking, dark-eyed young man was in love with Leda.

From that summer – or one following – I remember aunt Irene's hair-do.

Sometimes I would see her sitting in front of her dressing-table mirror in the main bedroom. The mirror gave back the reflection of her pale face and her arms as they struggled to wind her hair into a bunch behind her neck. I heard Leda saying: "Mama, have your hair cut. It's high time you cut your hair."

One morning my aunt's hairdresser, signora Gisella, came over and the house was immediately a-bustle. Leda leafed through the fashion magazines and showed them to Gisella who was arranging her combs, scissors, curling-irons and little burner in front of the mirror. With a worried look, my aunt was getting her drape ready. When she sat in front of the looking-glass and Gisella began to undo her hair, Leda took me by the hand and we went into the pantry. After what seemed to me like an extremely long time, Gisella called us; the two women were on their feet and my aunt looked rather red, as if from running, and kept feeling her neck with her long fingers.

Leda, almost before she looked at her, cried out: "Mama, you're a new woman. You've shed ten years. It's fantastic."

Gisella showed her approval, smiled and said: "D'you

see? D'you see how well it looks?"

Leda's cousins, Emma and Lola, turned up, from their home opposite. They burst into exclamations of amazement and kept crying out: "You really have shed ten years, aunty. You're a modern woman now."

My aunt smiled and said slowly: "It will be easier, certainly, especially in the morning, I'll be quicker;" but she still kept feeling her neck. I too couldn't stop looking at her nape, which seemed different, smaller, and I was really quite sorry that I could no longer see her round chignon, always slightly loose, and her hairpins forever about to fall out.

On Christmas Eve, the family gathered for the great dinner at Emma and Lola's house. Their house was large and welcoming. So many people called, if only briefly, to exchange greetings and good wishes. They would open the front door, you'd feel a gust of chilly air and someone crying out: best wishes, best wishes to all.

Often, for that occasion, the young folk who had gone overseas would return from their travels across the oceans. When they asked them: what do the Chinamen look like? What do pagodas look like? they'd smile and shake their heads.

It was one Christmas that my cousin Carlo Maria brought a mah-jong set as a present. We were waiting for dinner, the house was full of life, and the extended dinner-table occupied almost the whole of the dining-room. While we were waiting, we settled down in the work-room and started building the Great Wall of China. My cousin Carlo Maria said: this is the green dragon, this is the white dragon; Leda handed me the pieces and I, before setting them up, clasped them briefly in my hand because I liked their smooth and fragrant feel.

Emma and Lola often came to have coffee with us, aunt Irene was pleased to see them and I was pleased, too, though the two girls overawed me with their forthright manner and their loud laughter. After coffee, we'd all go for a siesta in the main bedroom which wasn't otherwise in use. Lola would take off her sun-dress and say, as she flung herself on to the bed: "I've had such a long bathe, enormously long. I must get some sleep."

She would fall asleep at once and slumber without stirring, looking like a statue, with her well-formed arms and dark face with high cheekbones that stood out against the bedsheets.

Emma and Leda would undress in leisurely style and stay in their slips. They'd sit up at the dressing-table, chattering away in an undertone, compare waists and bosoms and occasionally break into subdued laughter. Leda, ever smiling, would glance at me, who was supposed to be resting on the couch at the foot of the double bed, and say: "Why aren't you asleep, little one?"

I would shut my eyes to please her, but I would be wide awake. I liked being there, I liked the half-light, the sleeping girl and the girls not sleeping and that rural silence: from time to time through the half-closed shutters would come a breath of sea-air and someone's voice calling distinctly.

I remember once, all of a sudden, I squeezed Leda's hand and told her: "I do love you."

It must have been at the end of summer, probably near the day when I would have to leave and return home to town.

So I said: Leda, I do love you. I said it aloud and it was extraordinary that I managed to say it. Leda looked at me, smiled. She said: "I am glad." She mused for a moment, shook her head and added: "You love me now, while you're here. This winter, when you're at home back in town, you'll have forgotten me."

I felt let down: how could she not believe what I said? I objected in a burst of astonishment and anger that lasted that entire day. But the incident stuck in my mind, because a few months later, hearing my mother mention her, I realized that Leda had been at least partly right and that my memory of her was fading.

From time to time during the summer we'd go for the day to Emma and Lola's place in the country. We nearly always made the trip in Emma's boat. Male and female friends and relatives would join the party, only aunt Irene would always find one excuse or another and stay behind.

The two sisters' estate in the country covered a few hectares, the landward side under vines, the seaward strip covered by a grove of young pines.

After lunch we'd laze in the shade under the pine trees. The girls chatted away, while the young men sat apart in silence.

It was during one of these lazy afternoons that Emma described how she had got engaged. She'd gone off as a winter guest of some relatives in Lombardy and there she had met the family friend, a man older than herself, but kind and pleasant. This gentleman had visited more and more often during her stay there and, before she left, had asked her simply whether she too felt something special and, if so, whether he could come over and meet her parents.

As she told her story, Emma laughed quietly and in laughing her long blue eyes almost closed up. She said: "And I said, yes. I said yes to him straight away. Where did I find the courage, where on earth did I find it, I ask myself?"

And she looked round at her friends, who in turn looked smilingly at her: they had huddled round her in a ring and sat there thoughtfully and seemed to float weightlessly in that greeny–blue atmosphere.

Leda's closest friend was called Haydée and was the loveliest girl I had ever seen. When she came to see us, Leda was happy, excited even, and would get some coffee ready and tidy up the pantry.

The two girls would sit facing one another, I would sit

beside my cousin and gaze untiringly at her friend. Haydée would tittle-tattle, moving her head as she spoke and laughing. It was as if beauty played in ever-changing and mysterious patterns on her face. I hung on her words, her musical laughter, her bright glances and I felt they were continually hinting at some deeper secret which eluded me.

No one said so openly – but I knew – that my cousin Carlo Maria was hopelessly in love with her.

Nearly always before supper, Leda took me with her on a long walk along the sea-side promenade. On one side were ranged the cafes, families sitting round marble-topped tables, illuminated street-lamps, their light reflected from the wall-mirrors inside the cafes. On the other side was sea, black in the night, the silhouettes of vessels, swaying if the water was choppy, old and young strolling slowly along, up and down, engulfed in that swathe of semi-darkness. Nearly everybody knew everybody else and exchanged greetings and snippets of news.

It frequently happened that Leda would join a group: she'd let go of my hand, she'd laugh and chat, and I would be left half a step behind her and feel a weight upon my heart. I didn't like Leda during those moments and whenever anybody addressed me I'd reply in an undertone or pretend not to have heard, I'd look at the ground and think: anyway, I don't know you and I don't want to know you.

So we'd await the arrival of the ferry. At the sound of its high-pitched hooter with its periodic blasts announcing its approach, many people hastened towards the pier, while others carried on towards home.

One evening, while the ferry was berthing and we stood there watching the manoeuvre and spotting the arrivals – a brisk *borino* was blowing and the waves were almost coming over the pier – among the descending passengers I saw Paolo. He was wearing a light suit and his black hair looked glossier than ever. I looked anxiously to see whether he would glance in our direction, I looked at Leda and felt like tugging at her arm and saying to her look who's there, but Leda's eyes seemed fixed on the ship's bow and she stood there, motionless, without saying a word, while the wind ruffled our hair.

In the sunshine we often met count Gerardo in his broad-brimmed Panama, his white suit and black tie in mourning for his long-dead mother. He would raise his hat and lay his left hand on his heart in greeting but never stopped to talk to anybody, and there were murmurings about him. When we returned home Leda would recount these meetings and how the count had greeted her and how high he had held up his hat, and she laughed as she held her arm in the air, but aunt Irene was sorry for him: "Poor Gerardo. He's forty and still unmarried."

Leda protested: "All you think about is marriages and grandchildren. You think there's nothing else in the world."

My aunt would give her a crestfallen look and walk out of the pantry. Then I would ask Leda: "How old are you?"

"Twenty-five," she'd reply. "Yes, twenty-five, yes. I'm an old maid now."

She seemed sad for a moment, then brightened up again, smiling and humming: *We go diving for pearls in the depths of the sea – We have the world's finest diamonds, have we.*

Leda often scolded her mother, saying: come on, come down to the sea-side, come on, we'll wait for you.

"And what about lunch?" my aunt would reply. "Will the lunch cook itself?"

Leda would laugh and answer: "We'll just have a roll."

"A roll?" my aunt would retort, put out. "But the little one must have a meal. Lunch is important."

In fact, lots of good things came out of that kitchen – croissants for breakfast, home-made pasta, *polenta* soup, roast joints. Occasionally my aunt would pick out her cookery book and hand it to me.

"Read," she would say, "and choose the recipe you like best."

I'd leaf through the book and felt responsible for the choice I was going to make, I was pleased and nervous at one and the same time. The first time I chose a fluffy *torta Paradiso* and my aunt made it for me.

My cousin Carlo Maria sometimes chanced along to supper in the evening. He was on holiday, too. During the day he'd go on long cycle rides, and in the evening he'd tell us what he'd seen.

"The grapes promise well this year. Uncle will have a good crop. I met his daughters at the cafe."

"Will you come to the sea with us," Leda asked him. "Why don't you?"

He mused a while, then replied: "I see the sea all the rest of the year. So I prefer the countryside."

My aunt looked at him with affection and, I thought, with a touch of sadness.

One day when he and I were alone I asked him: "Do you like it at sea?"

He replied: "It's my job."

It only happened a couple of times. Coming back home, we found aunt Irene sitting motionless in the pantry, almost in darkness, her face ashen, her eyes almost veiled.

Leda was upset, she cried out: "What are you up to, mama? Why don't you move, what are you doing here all by yourself?"

She ran round turning on all the lights, called the house-maid and reprimanded her: can't you see, don't you care about the signora?

My aunt bit her lips. Then, with tears in her voice, she said: "I don't know. I don't know. I was thinking, and got frightened."

In the morning Emma and Lola would call to invite us to go boating with them. We'd bathe off an islet, little more than a rock, opposite the town. Lola was a skilful sailor. Like a lad, she'd rig up the boat, leap aft and forrard, she knew winds and currents. When we had a breeze the crossing was swift, but in calm weather it took us forever to cross that narrow stretch of water. Then the girls would lie back in the bottom, with their faces turned up to the sun, letting the waves rock them gently. They often sang, either old songs or current hits, and they knew an enormous number.

Sometimes Leda would break off, look at me and ask: "And what about you, little one, why aren't you singing?"

I replied: "I can't sing. And besides, I don't know the songs."

Leda immediately took up her song again in her contralto voice. We often crossed the ferry's path and then Emma would cry: "Take care, little one, we'll be dancing now. Hold tight, you're not a sailor."

The ferry went by, its wake tossed our boat up, the girls laughed. I smiled, too: I'd look at my cousins, I'd look at the sea, at the shore dressed in green pines and vines. Then my heart was full of peace, and for a while there was an end to that subtle anguish which I felt whenever I was among adults.

One afternoon Emma suddenly said: "Shall we make some candle-wax figurines? Shall we?"

I looked at her uncomprehendingly, but curious. My cousins, full of excitement, pulled out a boxful of Christmas candles and started melting them down on the gas-ring.

"Lock the door with the key," said Lola. "Aunty mustn't see us."

When the wax had melted to the right consistency, the girls started shaping it quickly. Emma was the most skilful, out of her hands came figures, trees and flowers, and when her figurine was all but complete, she'd insert the wick in the right place. Once the molten wax had all been used up, the girls arranged the figures on the marble tops of the bedside tables beside the double bed. Leda leapt up to close the shutters. Emma and Lola swiftly lit the little candles. In a moment the two bedside tables were glowing like diminutive altars. The red outdid the other colours and gave out a warmth and preciousness of tone. I had gone close to one of the little tables, but Leda stretched out her hand and drew me on to the bed, saying gently: "Mind your hair, little one. You'll catch fire."

The other two girls had also flung themselves on to the bed and in that glow their bare arms looked golden. I leant against Leda, who stroked me, and we all of us together lay there admiring the little flames, the dark shadow at their centre, the almost white halo around the edges, the candles burning down fast, petals and hands dripping.

Afterwards, for many days, we kept saying to each other: do you remember how pretty our figurines were? And I would ask anxiously: shall we make some more? Shall we? But we never did again.

Composition with dark centre

The invalid gestured down the long corridor and said: "Shall we go along to the visitors' room?" She went up to her friend, squeezed her arm and went on: "I'm so glad you're here."

Her eyes looked larger than usual that day in her drawn face. Her lineaments are dissolving, thought Olga as she looked at her, they're becoming. She drove the thought away, smiled and said: "I find you look well, Adina."

Ada shook her head and replied: "I don't know, I can no longer understand anything. The doctors won't explain, they're so evasive." She got upset and carried on: "I ask them direct questions. I have the right to know, haven't I?"

Olga replied at once: "But you must have patience. The doctors won't anticipate a diagnosis until they're certain. That's how it is."

Ada gave her friend a steady look and seemed relieved. She too smiled and said: "Yes, yes, maybe it's as you say."

They entered the great visitors' lounge with its sets of armchairs covered in green plastic and large metal ashtrays.

"Shall we sit near the window?" asked Ada and headed for the side of the room that was almost entirely plate glass and, being very high up in the building, showed a great rectangle of open sky and the dark canopy of pine trees.

They sat down facing one another. Olga gazed at her friend for a moment, banished all anxiety, every concern that was not uplifting and said, still smiling: "You know, I've done some sums, we've known each other for nearly thirty years. But we lost touch for a long time. The first time I saw you, you were wearing a light green dress and your eyes were green too."

Ada tossed her head back and laughed with pleasure: "I haven't got green eyes," she said, "though one of my brothers has."

Olga interrupted her, repeating: "But I tell you, they were green. You were walking in, talking loudly, you were very vivacious and you came up close to us."

They laughed, and their minds pursued the picture – Ada walking into a cafe and talking loudly, the two girls shaking hands and something happened.

Some of Ada's colleagues and her headmaster somewhat hesitantly came into the room. As soon as they saw her, they moved towards Ada, who rose to her feet, flushed with pleasure, and exclaimed: "You too, headmaster."

"My dear," said the headmaster, "my dear," and embraced her warmly.

The party had settled themselves around a glass–topped table. The headmaster listened attentively to his teacher's description of the symptoms of her illness. Finally Ada said: "I'm very tired of it all. They've kept me here so many months now, almost seven. It's far too long, isn't it?"

A middle-aged man, rather short and stumpy with an owl's round face, had entered the room. He dithered on seeing the group, approached them with short steps and said quietly to Ada: "I don't want to disturb you, I've come to hear your news."

"Thank you, ingegnere," replied Ada in an undertone, motioning him to a free seat. "Do take a seat." And she immediately turned her attention back again to her colleagues. "I would so like to ask you about school," she said, "even though it will make me feel sad."

The headmaster began relating recent school history with a wealth of detail. His voice, despite his age, was steady and incisive. While the headmaster was speaking, the man with the round head blew his nose, turned red in the face and almost at once got up, mumbling excuse me, excuse me.

There was a moment's silence, the headmaster raised his eyes and appeared to be contemplating the departing man in surprise.

"Who's he?" asked a female colleague, with a nod in the man's direction.

Olga answered quietly: "An engineer. A family friend."

Her colleague looked at Ada and gave a sigh: "We are your family. See how many of us there are?"

The light had diminished as a slight haze had shut out the sky. One of Ada's colleagues fished out a parcel and said hastily: "Ada, I'm going to your room, I must put away your nighties."

"Thanks, Michi," said Ada. "Thanks, you remember everything, you do."

As her colleague was leaving, the man came back into the room and came and took a seat beside Olga. Ada gave him a questioning look and the man said: "Excuse me. I had a bad nose-bleed. Perhaps I blew too hard, but that's me, I go at everything too hard." And he gave a forced laugh.

The ladies also smiled faintly while Ada looked away and appeared to ignore him. Olga rose to her feet and said: "I really have to go, but I will be back soon."

The man also got up and said quickly: "I'm coming too, if you don't mind. My very best wishes, signora Ada."

Olga and the man traversed the long corridor in silence. As they waited for the lift, the man said: "Do you remember? We met about a year ago at the station. I had come to see off Adina, who was leaving with you for the mountains. She was so pleased to be travelling with you." He took out his handkerchief and dried his eyes. He said: "I could see she wasn't her former self of late and I kept telling her: go and see a doctor, get yourself a check-up. But she's never heeded anything I've told her."

Olga sighed, and said, without looking at him: "I'm sure you're wrong, quite sure."

They entered an already packed lift and descended to the ground floor squashed in among the rest. Their goodbyes were brief as evening had fallen.

Ada's new room-mate sat up on her bed and said, looking at Olga: "There's nothing wrong with me, you know? There's never been anything wrong with me and I don't want to hear any sick talk."

She lifted up her hazel eyes, which were bulging because of thyroxtoxicosis, and said: "I used to be as fit as a fiddle. Even now the thermometer shows a fraction of a degree over, but I don't feel feverish. I could go about my usual business. If it weren't for my husband I certainly wouldn't be in here."

Ada, who was watching Olga impatiently, threw off her

77

bed–clothes and said aloud: "I'm hot. The heat in this room is stifling. Please open the window, Olga."

The other patient pursed her thick lips and butted in: "I'm not feeling hot, in fact I'm almost cold." She drew her long white legs out of the bed, searched with her feet for her slippers, got up and said: "I'll have a bath. If my husband turns up, I'll be in the bathroom." She walked elegantly across the room and said not another word.

There was a moment's silence. When the woman had closed the bathroom door behind her, Olga looked at Ada with a smile and asked: "Is there anything you'd like?"

Ada blushing slightly, said: "She irritates me, you know? She won't have this, she won't have that, she won't have the window open. If she feels cold, why doesn't she cover herself? You see the way she goes around? She wears the flimsiest garment for a nightie, showing all she's got. When her husband and children come to see her, they hold her hands and she stares and stares at them like a serpent, as if she were going to devour them."

Olga approached the plate–glass window and turned a handle so as to admit some fresh air from above. She came back to Ada's bedside and said: "Is that better?"

A puff of fresh air from the window brought in a whiff of springtime. Ada seemed to sniff the air, she said: "I'm so tired of being in here. And then her presence exasperates me. You know, Olga, since she's moved in here I've been feeling worse?"

Olga sat down beside the bed and replied: "Come on, don't look at her. You'll see, she'll be out of here soon. She'll vanish in just the same way as she appeared."

Ada, somewhat consoled, looked at her friend and said: "I hope so, I really hope so." She saw Olga was slipping on her jacket and added hastily: "Stay a little longer." Her eyes were shining, bright and soft. "I would like you to come every day. I get lots of visits, but you're the only one I long to see."

Olga sat down again and said honestly: "I like being with you, too."

The air was almost summery and the sunset glow cheered up the room. Olga smiled and said: "When you've recovered, we'll take a trip, go to the sea–side together and bathe as we used to."

They took their beach-bags and walked off together along the sea-front. On one side was the sea, the piers, the ferry-boats, on the other were the palaces with their statues, their gilt, their Gothic windows. There was a wind blowing and the two girls walked side by side, their fresh, sun-tanned arms brushed against each other, they narrowed their eyes, smiling.

Ada clutched Olga's arm and said: "D'you know, Olga? Yesterday evening my brother rang me from Brazil." She was breathing heavily, there was disquiet in her eyes and she suggested: "Let's stroll along the corridor, shall we? I need to move."

Olga nodded, grasped the arm which Ada had threaded through her own and enquired: "So, what have you got to tell me? How is your brother?"

Ada took some time to answer, sighing and saying to herself: "He rang me from Brazil. Imagine, from Brazil." She seemed to be collecting her thoughts, then began to explain: "Renzo's been out there for twenty-seven years and in all that time he's never rung me: too much emotion, he kept saying in his letters, too many things you can't say over the phone." She stopped, holding back her friend, deep distress showing on her face. She went on: "I hardly even recognized Renzo's voice on the phone, which shook me. I listened, spoke and at the same time wondered: is it I that don't remember it any more, have I forgotten my brother's voice? Or is it that his voice has changed so much?"

"But is he happy?" asked Olga. "Is he at least happy he went out there?"

The two friends had resumed walking up and down the corridor. They could hear the medicine trolleys swishing along and the nurses' loud voices. Two nuns walked swiftly past, and an orderly carrying a bunch of lilies. Ada reflected: "I don't think so. Perhaps he realizes it was a mistake. When he went to Sao Paolo the situation here was changing and if he'd stayed, with his good degree, who can tell. My poor brother. Now he's upset about me. Cobalt treatment, he kept asking, but is it really true that they're giving you cobalt treatment? In the end I had to cheer him up and explain that I'm not that poorly."

They entered the visitors' lounge, which was deserted, and sat beside the window. Ada rested her head on the back of her armchair and said: "About a year ago I had a visit from an Italo–Brazilian couple who were friends of theirs. I invited them home and they were very sweet and affectionate. But I gathered from the conversation that they were mainly my sister-in-law's friends. They didn't say much about my brother. I remember the wife telling me: your brother is very reserved, not at all like you, and sometimes it's hard to know which way to take him. Since then I've suspected that he feels isolated even from his family, that his wife and children don't understand him." She looked up and went on: "He and I have always exchanged long letters, up to eight or nine pages long. Renzo writes a good letter, he tells me so much about life out there, his impressions and hopes, but, my dear, inevitably, everything is veiled by the distance between us."

They looked at each other in silence. Each of them was mentally coursing through time and space.

"Why have you never paid him a visit?" asked Olga.

"I don't know. I kept putting it off."

The hospital friar entered, in a rush as usual. He bowed to the two ladies and said: praised be Jesus Christ. He looked at Ada and asked: "Is everything going smoothly, dear sister?"

"Thank you, father," Ada answered politely, "I do feel better today."

The friar cast an eye on Pirandello's novel *The Late Mattia Pascal*, which Olga had laid on the table, hesitated, then joined his hands together and said: "Ah, Pascal, a great philosopher."

Ada and Olga exchanged glances: both of them got the giggles and, just as when they were girls, each put a hand to her mouth, trying to stifle their laughter.

Michi looked apprehensively at her colleague and asked: "Are you feeling a little better?"

Ada gave a slight nod but did not open her eyes.

Her fellow-teacher looked round at Olga, who had just turned up, and whispered: "It's been very bad. It happened last night. It's lucky Professor Elia was around: as soon as he noticed she'd turned blue, he rushed to give her heart massage. By the time the nurses arrived, the real danger was over."

Ada opened her eyes, seeking Olga, and gave her a smile. Olga came up to her and stroked her on the shoulder. Ada said slowly: "D'you see the tricks this stupid illness plays on me?"

Olga replied: "It's over now. You'll feel much better tomorrow."

Another colleague who'd heard of Ada's crisis came in. She greeted her affectionately and said: "I came right away, I wanted to see you. You probably feel over-crowded."

Ada made a gesture of denial, and did not speak because of the effort. She was very pale, but even in its pallor her face was beautiful, with great tragic eyes and pronounced cheekbones.

Michi tidied up her bedside table, gave her a fresh supply of water, opened the drawer and checked that she had a napkin and cutlery, and said: "Everything's in order." She turned to her invalid colleague and added quietly: "I've paid the rent and collected your mail from home. There was just a small bill."

Olga looked at her and said with enthusiasm: "You're splendid – so thoughtful."

Ada breathed: "What would I do without you?"

The woman laughed and said: "Go on, what nonsense, I won't hear such talk."

Professor Elia arrived. He looked at once grave and mild. Olga smiled at him as if he were an old friend, though in fact she had only heard of him from Ada and her friends. They exchanged a few words, then Olga said in a low voice: I'll be off, there are too many of us here, but I'll be back tomorrow.

Outside the door of Ada's room, the figure of the engineer could be seen pacing to and fro. From time to time he appeared at the door, his eyes enquiring: how is she? Signora Michi or whoever would reassure him and the man would withdraw into the corridor and carry on pacing and smoking unceasingly.

Olga took the seat beside the bed and said: "We're on the mend, aren't we?"

Ada smiled and replied: "I'm better, but weak."

Olga looked at her friend, hesitated an instant and said: "The engineer sends his greetings. He was so insistent that I should tell you he's rung up every day and is very concerned."

Ada gazed at the ceiling without replying. Olga cleared her throat and continued: "He told me he'd come much more often, only you have so many visitors and he doesn't know whether it gives you pleasure. He doesn't want to do anything to annoy you."

Ada remained silent, then said: "I don't care whether he comes. I don't care a bit about seeing him."

Olga lowered her eyes and replied: "Why do you talk like that? He's fond of you."

Ada hitched herself up a trifle against her pillows and said: "But I haven't cared for him for ages. His presence doesn't bring me pleasure – far from it. When I see him, I always have the same thought in my mind, that I wasted years and years on him, because my husband had left me and he said he loved me so much and showered me with attention. But he would never leave his family."

She slumped down again on her pillows and the hollows round her eyes had gone deeper and bluer. She went on: "We were always hiding away. I was distraught to think that someone at the school might find out, especially the headmaster, who thought so highly of me. At that time I was being pestered by nuisance calls at night and I could never work out whether they had anything to do with that affair or whether they were coincidental. I was often woken up at dead of night, sometimes the person at the other end murmured obscenities and laughed, at other times there was just silence."

The nurse came in and checked the medical chart. Ada

followed her with her eyes, waited till she left, seemed to brush aside her reminiscences and said: "Tell me about yourself, Olga. How are things? How are your children?"

Olga passed a hand across her forehead, collected her thoughts and said: "Fine. Pretty well."

Ada gave her a close look and pressed her: "Really well?"

"Sure."

"You don't look happy. Is something bothering you?"

"Who hasn't got worries?"

"Oh," Ada broke in with sudden vigour. "You're lucky. You have a good marriage and you don't know how much that means. You must be happy. When I think of you."

"I am happy," said Olga slowly. She bent towards the bed and added. "Everything's fine. Only, you know, when your children have grown up. But everything's fine, don't worry."

As she crossed the main hall, Olga spotted Professor Elia. He was waiting for the lift and his intense features stood out among the crowd. Olga waved him a greeting and the professor, catching sight of her, gave an answering nod; for an instant Olga met his piercing gaze. She left the hospital amid a stream of people and immediately looked upwards: a black, almost solid, cloud of swallows darkened the sky and their twittering, thought Olga, was not cheerful.

A good-looking lad was leaning against the broad window, his eyes dark and sad, his features regular.

"You know, Olga, that's my nephew," said Ada. He's Luca, my brother Rosario's boy. It was so long since we last met." She looked sad for a moment.

The lad made an expressive gesture and said: "The last time we met was at the station in Florence, just by chance, a couple of years ago. Do you remember? I looked up and who do I see at the window in front of me but my aunt Ada just about to leave."

Ada gave a happy smile and said: "You called out: aunt Ada, aunt Ada, and I rushed to the carriage door. We only just managed a hug."

"I was on my way to Turkey, it was my last long trip. I stayed four months."

"Yes. And I was on my way to Provence with a school party." For a moment Ada seemed engrossed and said: "That was a lovely trip, I remember it was always sunny." She collected herself, gave her nephew a searching look and asked him: "Tell me, Luca, how are things? Are you more settled now?"

Olga, too, looked at Luca with interest. The young man left the window, stopped and replied: "Oh, yes, aunty, pretty well."

"What about your work?" enquired Ada apprehensively. "How are you getting on with your work? Are you enjoying it?"

Luca knitted his thick, dark eyebrows and said: "I'm teaching again. I've got a temporary post for this year. After that, we'll see."

He'd glanced at his watch and looked embarrassed. Olga came to his rescue and said: "You've got to be off, it's such a long way to the station."

Luca nodded quickly, came up to the bed, gave his aunt a quick hug, and said: "I really do have to go. Goodbye, aunt Ada. I will be back soon, though, I promise."

When the lad had gone, Ada half shut her eyes, laid her head back on the pillows and a happy little smile played upon her face.

"Do you see, Olga?" she said in a low voice. "He came for my sake. He came to see me."

"He's so handsome," said Olga warmly. "And nice, too, I think."

Ada concurred: "He's like his father. Perhaps even more good-looking, but I thought my brother Rosario was especially handsome."

She was silent, smoothing down the edge of the sheet with her small hands. It was the rest period, and the half-shut Venetian blinds made the room dim.

Ada started and said: "Do you know what my husband used to say? He used to say I was in love with my brother. I used to get angry and he would insist I was really in love even without realizing it. Do you remember the kind of man Lucio was? Morbid, manic, he used to get a kick out of baiting and tormenting me. During those short, terrible years of our marriage I had a recurring dream: we were in a zone outside space, colourless, Lucio stood in front of me with his arm raised, pointing out to me a couple making love. I couldn't see them, but I knew they were there and I couldn't help picturing their actions, while Lucio kept egging me on to look at them and laughed, then turned back towards me and I discovered that his features were changing, it wasn't Lucio any more but my brother Rosario and I was aghast, but I also felt joyful and my heart was beating so fast that I would wake up."

They looked at each other in consternation for some while. Olga murmured: "Good God, what strange dreams one has sometimes."

She stretched out her hand and stroked Ada's arm. She went on in a lighter tone: "I met Rosario at your wedding. I remember him: he was tall with copper-red hair. He wasn't like the rest of you."

Ada smiled, her eyes gleamed. "He was tall," she said with pride. "He was the best-looking of us all. He went to study in Milan and started working there and got married."

Olga got up and said: "It's time for your injection."

The voices of the nurses and the squeaking of the trolley could be heard coming along the corridor.

Ada desultorily rolled up her sleeve and said: "For what it's worth."

Olga arrived to find Ada just finished her meal. She'd been picking at her food and there were remains of chicken and vegetables on the dishes.

"Aren't you hungry today?" asked Olga. "Wouldn't you like something else?"

"No, no," said Ada. "Sit down, talk to me."

Olga hesitated, then said: "It's warm out now." She encountered a dejected look and hurried on to say: "I met Professor Elia on my way up. He must be outside the common run of people."

Ada nodded repeatedly. She pushed back her tray and echoed: "Oh, yes, he's no ordinary person. What made you realize that?"

Olga chuckled. "I wonder. It must be intuition."

"Poor Elia, he's had a frightful life," Ada said. "He was sent to Dachau during the war, his mother was Jewish and she was taken by the Germans. So Elia gave himself up and asked to follow her to the same camp. So he managed to save her. When they came back, he'd become a Catholic. He never talks about that period, though. I've known him for nearly twenty-five years, all the time I've been a tenured teacher. He teaches natural sciences, but he also has a degree in philosophy. At first, we didn't talk much, he overawed me. It was when my husband went off that we became friends. His desertion left me stunned, I still get mental blanks and palpitations at night."

Olga leaned towards the bed and said gently: "Tell me some more about Elia."

Ada livened up again: "When we were finishing work at the same time, Elia would wait for me on his scooter. He'd never say: I'll be waiting for you, but I'd come out of school and know he was there. I'd get on behind him and hold on tight. Now that I think about it, it was fun to cross town like that. When we got near where I lived – I was at the Prati then – he'd stop, hand me my books, we'd compare notes about our year, about the syllabus. We often used to meet at concerts. He really understands music. In the early years he came alone, then he started bringing his eldest son. Some of my colleagues used to say; he's in love with you, don't you see the way he looks at you? I don't think he was, he never said anything to me that could lead me to think so. He held me in esteem, that's true. And I hold him in esteem and regard him as a noble man."

There was a knock at the door and a girl appeared. She wore a mini-skirt, had a bag slung over her shoulder, her face was bright.

"Oh, Fausta," said Ada, and she held out her arms. "I'm so pleased to see you."

The girl bent forward over the bed and kissed her teacher. "I'm pleased to see you, too," she said. "Yes, I am pleased." She looked round in sudden impatience and said: "But why are you still here, signora? We're waiting for you, you know. We're longing for you to come back."

Ada seemed upset, then said: "Olga, this is Fausta Dandi. She's a bright pupil, I've had her since first form. What about your dancing?" she said, turning to the girl again. "How's your dancing going?"

Fausta tossed her head and her hair undulated gracefully. She laughed and replied promptly: "Oh, the dancing's going fine. I've made enormous progress lately. Who knows, I might really turn into a dancer" She frowned and went on: "I wouldn't like to teach or do anything else, I'd really like to be able to dance." She drew herself up and seemed set for a little flight.

Olga looked at her fondly and thought, dear god, these young people. She said: "Good for you, Fausta, at least you know what you want."

"My friend has two children of her own," explained Ada.

They heard the voice of the doctor coming on his afternoon round.

"We'll step out for a moment," said Olga. "We'll wait outside."

They stood outside the half-open door. The corridor was deserted. The girl looked at the woman, her eyes darkened and she said: "But why's the signora still here?" She looked round, raised her eyebrows disapprovingly at the place and persisted: "Why doesn't she go back to her own home? She'd be much more comfortable there, I'm sure of it. Don't you agree, signora? Don't you think so too?"

Olga gazed into the distance and said: "Of course, Fausta, of course."

Ada watched Michi out of the room, her bulging bag, her brisk gait. She said: "I don't know what I'd have done without Michi. She's seen to everything right from the start, she applied for my admission, she looks after my flat, she deals with the bills."

"She's splendid," said Olga. "She's a wonderful friend."

Ada seemed to reflect for a moment, then repeated vigorously: yes, that's right. She bent her head and said quietly, but in a voice that came from deep inside her, vibrant: "And yet, Olga, do you know? There was a time when I didn't trust Michi." She nodded several times and repeated: "I didn't trust her, and, if you'd like to know the whole truth of the matter, I was convinced there was malice behind that nice face of hers."

Olga looked at her in surprise and couldn't help exclaiming: "But what are you saying, Ada?"

"Oh, yes," returned Ada, "Oh, yes. We first met at the school and became friends. I was at my ease with her, we talked a lot – about our pupils, about teaching, and, as we got closer, about quite private matters. It wasn't until later that I realized, quite suddenly, that Michi ardently desired everything I had. Or rather, she wanted to be me, even to have my emotions. I'd say my mother and she'd say my mother, I was loved by my pupils and she wanted the same love, I translated Greek poetry and so did she."

Her cheeks were strongly flushed and her voice had turned almost into a hiss as she said this. "Oh," she said, "it's hard to explain, I'd always find her at my elbow, I felt I couldn't even breathe, I had this exasperating feeling that she somehow wanted to take my place, squeezing me out."

She hesitated, then resumed, almost trembling: "So now I think at times: here I am, she's got me in her power."

Olga jumped to her feet, took a deep breath, feeling a sense of oppression. She said: "I can't believe it. You might have got it wrong."

"Maybe," answered Ada. "Maybe. And now I'm full of remorse."

Olga chuckled nervously. She sat down again, and resumed: "We're a complicated pair, you and I. But that's why I enjoy listening to you."

Ada smiled too, and the tension subsided. She stretched out her hand and said: "I can tell *you* everything."

"What lovely flowers," said Olga, admiring a vase of carnations of different colours. "What a lovely bouquet." And she skilfully rearranged a few stems.

"Yes," said Ada, "they are beautiful." She looked at them pensively and eventually added: "*He* sent them."

88

"The engineer?" murmured Olga.

Ada nodded and rested her head against the pillows, which were piled high behind her. "At one time he never stopped sending flowers, my house was always full of roses, carnations, whatever was in season."

Olga sat at the foot of the bed and said: "He must have been very much in love."

Alda gazed at the red, mauve and pink blooms that looked like daubs against the wall and answered slowly: "Yes, he loved me. He always wanted to know where I was so that he could join me or simply watch me go past. He'd send me flowers and cards. Once, when we were travelling to Greece by ship, he telephoned me. A maritime telephone call. Michi was the only person who knew about us, she had a good laugh when I told her about that. A maritime telephone call, she said, just like a government minister."

Olga laughed out loud, too, and she continued: "He really does seem to be a kind, decent fellow."

Ada raised herself up a bit, her face was pale and strained and faint small freckles showed through the skin over the cheek-bones. Her eyes took on a sadness, a secret fire within them made them very beautiful. She said intensely: "But still, Olga, I'd have liked a different man. I wished I had someone different."

Olga bent her head and felt her cheeks turn hot. She'd met the engineer for the first time at the station. Ada was walking along briskly through the throng towards her with a smile and there was he, just a step behind, thick-set, round-headed, struggling under the weight of her suitcase. "He wanted to see me off." Ada was saying, "he insisted on coming. So now you're meeting him."

Olga dismissed the memory. She passed a hand through her hair and murmured: "Just think that he loved you."

Ada reached with her arm towards her friend, but said only: "How tired I am of being in here."

Olga and Michi emerged from Ada's room.

"Let's have some coffee," proposed Michi. "We can go up to the top floor and have a coffee at the bar." She laid her hand on Olga's arm and added: "That way we can take our minds off things for a bit."

When they were at the counter, they exchanged looks of relief. Michi had a graceful figure and her appearance was always neat. Olga said: "You're wearing a nice blouse, it suits you."

"I like clothes. But I have so little time, I do everything in a rush. Sometimes I wonder if it's fair on the children."

"These are special circumstances, though," said Olga. "Unfortunately, it won't always be like this."

"Right," replied Michi, "of course. Though I sometimes wish and hope it would go on forever. At least I can see her and speak to her."

They sipped at their coffee. There were some patients in dressing-gowns around, as well as visiting relatives. The plate-glass windows encompassed a great expanse of sky slightly tinged with pink, but grey streaks of cloud hid the horizon.

Michi put down her cup and said: "Do you know, Olga? The school isn't the same without her. She's always helped me, not only with my teaching, with the doubts one always gets, but because with Ada everything became interesting. She and I understood one another, it only took a glance. We did so much together. Once we took a school trip to Greece. It was the first time we'd been there, Ada was so excited and something extraordinary happened: she understood mod-ern Greek. I can still see her, laughing with joy and saying: I understand it all, I understand what they're saying. Now I'm bored at school, I've lost interest, I have no one to match up to."

Michi stood motionless, Olga went up to a free seat, she sat down and gazed at the sky which was changing colour and appeared, now that the sun had set, clear and remote. She looked at Michi standing there, her well-groomed hair, her regular features, almost perfect. Thoughts and ques-tions jostled together in her mind, but all at once she felt worn out, as though she were climbing up a long incline with no end in sight.

The bar had emptied and there was no one behind them except the woman rinsing out the glasses behind the bar.

Michi touched Olga's shoulder and said: "Aren't you feeling well?"

"No, no," answered Olga. "We'd better rejoin her, or she'll be fretting."

"Do stay, Olga."

"I can't. I have to go."

"Do sit just a while longer."

"I'll be late home and there are so many things to see to."

Olga sat down on the edge of the seat, her mind on the fact that if she were late that evening she wouldn't see her children, and repressed a gesture of impatience.

Ada held out her arm with outspread palm as if to ward off something and said: "This is the time when my dismal mood and horrid thoughts assail me." She turned her eyes, her despairing eyes towards the window. She continued: "I keep asking myself, I keep asking, will I get out of here?"

"But what are you talking about?" Olga almost shouted. "What are you thinking? You will be out of here, we'll be out of here and nothing will be left of this but a bad dream, and eventually, as with any dream, you'll forget it. It will all be over."

Olga left the room, turning with a smile just at the door. She stepped quickly along the corridor. She called the lift, which was a long time in coming. Another person had come up beside her to wait for it also. They both stood motionless before the lift gate and each of them let out a sigh. Before Olga's eyes was her friend's face. They were returning from a trip to the mountains and the coach was descending towards the plain in a long loop. They could see the gentle hills, the fruit trees, the deep green, the limpid sky and here and there coronets of little clouds rested on the mountain tops. The two of them were chatting away intensely as the coach sped on its way, but every now and then they would look up and tap each other on the arm in their pleasure at beholding that varied and charming scenery.

As they waited for Ada to return from the ground floor where she had been taken for some tests, her friends had settled themselves in the visitors' lounge. The sky was bright outside, but on account of its position, the lounge was plunged in vivid shadow and the figures and objects inside it were sharply outlined. The women had taken their seats quietly, hands joined on their laps, with absorbed expressions. One of the group was a young teacher who in her time had been a pupil of Ada's and had then become her friend. Viola was a girl with ash-blond hair, a sweet face, a trifle spoiled by a slightly receding chin, but her figure was firm and perfect. She said: "I visited the faculty today and I felt as if I was dreaming. It's been only ten years since I graduated and everything has changed so much. There are just a few of us students and there was plenty of room for us in the two little lecture-rooms. Now there's a mass of students and the atmosphere is one of great confusion. On my way back home I reflected about my teaching, which I started early in life with high hopes, but lately I've found work difficult. I don't find myself in tune either with the teachers or with the children, possibly because I'm neither young nor old. Anyway, I was surprised to catch myself facing the future with such a deep insecurity."

Olga would have liked to say something about her own eldest son, but Michi had started talking about her experiences with high-school pupils and was getting animated. She said: "Yes, these are difficult years, and sometimes one despairs. But I do think what's involved is very personal and perhaps everyone's got to sort it out as an individual. Ada thought that way, too."

"You reckon?" said Viola. "Do you really think so?" but she seemed engrossed, following her own train of thought.

Ada's nephew appeared in the doorway. The pallor of his face was striking. The ladies welcomed him festively. Michi asked at once: "How come you're here? We weren't expecting you."

The young man joined the group and explained: "I had a free day and thought I would come."

"You look tired," Michi went on. "Would you like to have something?" Luca gave her an appreciative look and said no, no. He put his bag down, took a seat and appeared to relax. He started relating: "There was an unexpected strike, the train was stuck for two hours. It was terribly hot and people became excited, they were shouting. They they calmed down, some of them fished out their sandwiches, their coffee-flasks, everyone was swapping eats." The lad became lively, a twinkle of amusement came into his eyes and he went on: "There was an elderly woman from the Veneto sitting opposite me. A nice woman, amusing. She wouldn't stop repeating that she was on her way to her brother-in-law's funeral, but that if she missed her connection then it would be goodbye to the funeral, she wouldn't make it in time. She even brought her husband into it, he just had a cold, nothing serious, and he'd refused to come, he wouldn't do his duty as a brother-in-law. And at this point the woman, staring us all in the face, kept asking: but is that right? What are we, dogs or Christians?"

Luca mimicked the woman and the ladies laughed at his story. The young man laughed too, and his face was no longer dismal.

A nurse beckoned to them from across the room to let them know that Ada was back in her room. They got up promptly and went to see her.

Viola was leaning against the white wall of the corridor waiting to enter.

"She's asleep," said Viola. "Ada's asleep."

"You didn't need to come," replied Olga in an undertone. "You live so far off."

Viola crinkled her forehead and answered: "Yes, it is tiring but I just had to. You know how it is." She gave a kind of start and her fine body stiffened. "I still can't come to terms with it, I find it impossible to believe. The news came to me so suddenly. This year, when I came back from my country holiday, I didn't get in touch with anybody. When I was informed, Ada was already in here."

They went slowly along the corridor. They passed some nurses who were laughing and joking. A nun appeared and said: silence, my daughters, silence: and she saw them off.

Viola resumed: "God, I just can't believe it. I began to cry and couldn't calm down."

They stopped again. Viola was pale, her forehead glistening.

"Meeting Ada meant a great deal to me," she said. "I was fifteen. I was withdrawn, apathetic. With her, I was transformed. I remember so many incidents from my high school days, so many days when we were preparing for our exams. Ada followed us almost morbidly, we girls were very keen to study, everything was alive. At that time Ada was already alone, her husband had gone abroad with another woman and I think this created a strong sense of solidarity between us. We felt she was close to us." She lowered her voice and added shyly: "I'm telling you all this because I feel as if I've known you for such a long time."

The two women looked at each other.

"Oh, yes," said Olga, "I feel I know you, too. Ada has often spoken to me about you."

The door to the room next to Ada's burst open and out came a merry young woman. Her companion was carrying her suitcase and a nurse was handing her her cape.

"Thank you," said the lady as she took it. "Thank you." On seeing Olga, she addressed her: "Do give my regards to your friend," she said. "Give her my very best regards. I'm going back home. You see? My husband's come for me. I'm off."

The little party headed towards the lift and their cheerful but subdued voices and their hurried steps on the floor-tiles receded along the corridor.

"You know, Olga? Stuck here in this bed, my mind goes back more and more to my birthplace and the years of my childhood and early adolescence. It was the same with my brother Rosario: towards the end he would dwell on little incidents in the past and when we were alone, he and I, all of a sudden he'd come out with some words in our dialect and he'd keep saying: d'you hear how well it sounds put that way, or, d'you remember how our mother . . . ?

So do I relish the sound of certain words and I suddenly

94

shoot back into our poor house almost without furniture which is precisely what made it so austere. After our father died, we escaped from that town to come up north, to start on a freer life and, as we thought, a fuller one. But, Olga, my dear, that small town which I thought had been wiped out is back in my mind now and I often stroll along that blue sea, so peaceful, I follow the road from house to the school and I can feel that touch of frost at Christmas-time when my brothers fetched out the box of terracotta figurines and set up the little crib I liked so much.

When we came up north – you and I met soon after – we didn't talk of home. Only my mother every now and then gave a sigh and said, as if it were a lament: up here isn't like our parts.

I dream of her sometimes."

Ada brought her hand up, tried to clear her voice, that had a catch in it, and said: "You remember how tiny she was, our mama?"

Ada was seated in the armchair in her room, wrapped in her olive-green dressing-gown, dark rings round her great eyes, her beautiful lips turned almost white.

Olga sat down on the edge of the bed, smiled at her and said: "Adina, do you know the first time I saw you? I mean before I met you. I saw you acting with the university group. The war was just over, everyone was up to something, people were travelling all over the place. So I came to that cinema-cum-theatre. The hall was long and narrow, packed with school-children, I'd found a seat in one of the back rows and there was a boisterous atmosphere because of the children. I remember you were on the left of the stage, you were standing next to your friend who was sitting down and you were delivering your last lines. The warm glow of a summer sunset was shining on you and I can still see your small round head, your well-judged gesture and I can still almost hear your gentle voice saying: we will rest, we will rest . . ." She broke off with a tender laugh: "Do you see how I remember you?"

Ada flushed with pleasure, blood flowed into her cheeks

and she instantly looked younger. She replied: "I was good, wasn't I?"

Olga nodded with conviction.

"A pity I didn't make anything of it," Ada sighed again, and her eyes darkened and she began to torment the bed-sheet. "Isn't it a pity?"

They looked at each other and opened channel upon channel into the past, channels of light and signs that had now become confused.

"That building," said Ada, "that theatre – it was by the sea, wasn't it?"

"Yes," said Ada, "by the sea."

Once again they were in that azure-gilt atmosphere. The goods train crawled along the harbour-front, people cried out or laughed.

Olga resumed: "I admired you greatly. That's why I was so pleased to meet you."

Ada looked affectionately at her friend, the bright depths in her eyes were visible again, she looked serene and murmured: "Do come again, Olga, do come, tomorrow even."

Olga saw Viola on the steps in front of the great entrance to the building. She was pale and her eyes were red-rimmed.

"I want to see you," said Viola. "I want to be with you." And she made a disconsolate gesture.

"It's the same with me," said Olga, "the same with me."

They embraced and parted quickly. It was raining, but the sky was bright and promised clear weather.

Michi tip-toed about Ada's room so as not to disturb her, as she seemed to be dozing. Olga stood still at the door for a moment, then whispered: "If you have to go, I'm here now."

The woman gave her friend a long look before breathing her reply: "Thank you." She moved towards Olga and added: "Tell her I'll be back tomorrow morning. Later on, Luca will be coming, too."

Olga, alone, sat on the armchair at the foot of the bed. Only a faint light filtered into the room, as the Venetian blinds were fully lowered. Ada was slumped on her pillows, her lean arms lying alongside her body, her small hands tapering and inert. Olga forced herself not to think: she gazed at the objects, the pencil of light that ran along the floor, the gleaming metal of the bedside table.

A nurse appeared at the door, glanced at the patient and went off.

Ada stirred. She opened her eyes, saw Olga, and said quietly: "I've been very ill, do you know?"

Olga nodded and replied: "I know, I know, they told me all about it. But you're better now."

Ada looked uncertain: "I don't think so, I really don't think so."

"Yes, yes, you'll see," repeated Olga. And she couldn't bring out any other words.

There was a long silence, then Ada said: "Please, open the window, I want to see the sunlight."

Olga went up to the window, made the Venetian blind spring up and the room was flooded with the glow of the sunset. Far away in the pink sky could be seen the tops of the pine trees and the darting swallows.

Olga resumed her seat. Ada murmured: "Elia was here, professor Elia."

"Don't speak," replied Olga, "you'll tire yourself; we'll speak tomorrow."

Ada closed her eyes. She awoke a few minutes later and said quickly: "Elia is a dear man, but in these last few days he's been at me. You know, Olga? At me. He talks to me about God, he faces me with problems I don't know."

A pang went through Olga's heart. She searched for words and said hastily: "Perhaps it's just that you and I aren't in the habit of facing certain questions." She blushed with the tension, and whispered: "Or perhaps we put them off, don't you think?"

Ada gave a little nod, seemed to be reflecting intensely, gazed at her friend with abandon, trust, love and murmured: "But I don't want to face those questions. D'you understand, Olga? I don't want to hear that kind of talk."

Olga bowed her head, took Ada's hand and stroked it just once gently. She said slowly: "Of course, of course."

They stayed like that in silence.

Ada had turned her head towards the window though which flowed a rapidly dwindling light.

Olga kept still so as not to disturb her friend and waited in anxiety, in longing and in grief for someone to turn up and relieve her.

In contemplating the moon

He lifted up the child and, pointing to the horizon over the sea, he said: "See, Lele? Lightning."

The child eyed his grandfather's mouth, appeared to concentrate with furrowed brow, and mouthed the word with an effort: "Lightly, grandpa?"

His grandfather laughed, kissed the child. Along the horizon heat-flares lit up the almost violet-coloured evening sky. A voice came through the trees, shouting: "Giunio, bring the child back. He's got to sleep."

The Professor acted deaf, hugged the little boy and muttered: "Us two shall go along the pier, shan't we?"

He strolled away along the pier which he'd had built nearly twenty years earlier for mooring his sailing-boat when he sailed from his little town on the coast to his property in the country. The pier reached out about thirty metres and one side of it had been used to form a tiny dock, a safe little haven.

Walking along, Giunio lifted up his face and said: "The wind's shifting. It might rain tomorrow."

The boy leaned forward, stretched out his arm and repeated: "Grandpa, lighty."

"Did you hear me?" said his wife loudly from a few paces distance. "Where are you off to, Giunio? The child has to sleep."

The Professor turned round and saw his wife, her large bosom heaving, her white hair gathered behind her neck.

"We're on holiday," he replied, and made a grimace. "You're always such a drag with your timetables."

"What on earth are you saying?" returned the woman. "Me?" She was about to answer back, at the same time felt humiliated by his words and besides didn't want to be seen to lose her temper in front of the child. So, while trying to keep calm, she began to move her head imperceptibly in reproof, and her husband, watching her, thought: she's act-ing like an old woman, she's old; and he thought this quite calmly, to his own amazement.

His wife raised her head and said in a low voice: "You really are a peasant."

Giunio shrugged slightly and made no reply. Then he asked: "Where's your daughter?"

"They're all in among the pines, Rita's dividing the water-melon."

The grandfather then kissed the child again and handed him over to his wife.

"Off you go," he said. "Off you go, Lele. Good night."

The woman took him into her arms and kissed him: "My treasure," she said in rapture, "you're your granny's treasure."

The infant looked at her anxiously: "Bed-time? Bed-time?" he asked. And he seemed on the verge of tears.

To divert him, his grandmother rocked him up and down on her arms singing ride-a-cock-horse.

She hugged the child and cherished the moment, but at the same time her mind dwelled resentfully on her husband, plaguingly: why does he do it? Why does he bait me? She could feel her temples perspire and reflected that the child was growing and was too heavy for her now.

Under the pine trees, on a rug spread out on the ground against the damp, Rita was slicing the water-melon, one slice for her husband, one for her cousin Vilma, and one for herself. They were squatting cross-legged in silence.

The man looked at his wife and his look was intense. But Rita's mind was elsewhere, she was humming as she munched.

Vilma broke the silence and cried out: "Look, there's a red streak along the horizon. It's beautiful."

Lino turned towards the sea and repeated: "Yes, it's beautiful." He looked again at his wife and said: "Did you see, Rita?" He put his arm around her shoulders, Rita started and the water-melon fell from her hands.

"God," she said, "I've soiled the rug. You've made me

soil the rug." And she stood up.

Lino also stood up, stepped forward and his eyes were troubled. At last he said: "I'm going to kiss the child good night. Will you come too?"

"No," said Rita. "For once, my mother's putting him to bed."

Lino walked stiffly off, his head upright, as was his wont. When he disappeared among the trees Rita smiled at Vilma and sat down again. She felt lighter and a sudden thought passed through her head: is it possible that his mere presence? She quickly dismissed the thought and, turning round, echoed: "Yes, it is a lovely sunset." She resumed her humming: "*Captain, Captain, there's a man in the brine, quickly, quickly, sling him a line.*" She laughed and said with a sigh: "God, when I think of that apartment in town."

"But you said it's large," said Vilma, amazed. "Don't you like town life?"

Rita did not answer. She lay down full length on the sheet and said: "I can see Venus right down there. Can you?"

So they remained peacefully for a while. Rita asked: "How long are you staying with us, Vilma?"

"I don't know, a fortnight, perhaps."

"You're skinny, but it suits you. Are you fifteen now?"

"In three months' time." Vilma moved closer to her cousin and started to chat. She wasn't quite at ease with these relatives whom she only saw in summer, but now Rita's questions had reassured her and she felt more comfortable. She said: "Yesterday, when I arrived, I was very tired, it was an exhausting journey, the coach was packed, some passengers had to stand."

Rita registered this with a nod and said: "I know those coach journeys, I've done them lots of times."

Vilma seemed struck by a thought and resumed: "People were very excited, everybody was talking and some of them kept saying there's going to be a war."

Rita darkened and her face looked smaller. She replied quickly: "Lino says there won't. He's a sea-captain, perhaps he understands a bit more than other people." For a moment she too thought of war as a real possibility. She thought of the child and of herself and was scared: "Oh," she exclaimed, "what a topic, let's talk about something else."

She could see, far away through the trees, her mother

emerge from the house and look at the sky and, immediately after, her husband coming back towards them, wearing a canvas hat against the damp night air.

She got up briskly and muttered: "There's something I've forgotten."

She ran off to the pier. It was almost dark now, there were only splashes of pink and violet along the horizon. She went the whole length of the pier and sat down at the end of it.

The pale crescent moon was rising slowly. The sea lapped against the rocks which protected that side of the pier, and white flecks of foam appeared round about. Rita forced herself not to think of anything. She wanted to enjoy that observation-post, which had always been hers. There were few fishing-boats in the distance and from time to time, soft and swift, a flash of lightning lit up the sky.

Lino knelt on the rug and glanced at the space where his wife had been. "I bet she's gone down beside the sea," he said. "I bet."

Vilma smiled a yes. She stroked her long hair and tried to think of something to say to this cousin of hers by marriage.

Lino, unobserved, was observing her. He smiled and started to talk. His voice was deep and his pronunciation distinct, accent-free. He said: "Last time I saw you was at my wedding, three years ago. You were still a child."

"Yes," said Vilma, and she was pleased to be talked about.

Lino went on: "From time to time I asked Rita for your news, even she often hadn't heard anything about you." His eyes narrowed, and he asked quietly: "Do you remember my wedding-day?"

Vilma nodded. Lino was squatting on the rug on his haunches and tugging at the edge. He sighed and said: "I'd just come back from East Africa and everyone treated me very affectionately, they spoiled me, even Rita."

Vilma feigned ignorance and said: "I'd never been to a wedding before, yours was the first. I remember everything, Rita's white dress, the church and all those people."

Lino appeared engrossed. He went on playing with the

rug, then said: "We've got the photographs of that occasion. And we have a photograph of our relatives and you are in the front row among the other children." He laughed and looked hard at her with his intense eyes. "Looking at that photograph, I've often thought that you were a special girl and out of all those people you were the only one I'd look at, I'd imagine you grown up, I'd wonder what you'd do, who you'd fall in love with."

Vilma listened with excitement. She always found it hard to speak, but she enjoyed this conversation and said happily: "I've got the same photograph. It shows us on our uncle's verandah and you and Rita are already in your travelling clothes."

Lino stretched himself out on the rug and went on: "It's strange, you're a full-grown girl now and the impression I had then just came back to me." He remained silent for a while, eyed his cousin and asked: "Have you got a boy-friend? Have you already been with him?"

Vilma made a gesture of surprise. She reddened and said: "Why?"

For a moment, their eyes met. Vilma got up and turned her back on him. Her heart was beating quite fast. She said: "I'm off," and started running through the pine trees.

The Professor saw Vilma coming across the clearing and called out to her. The girl hesitated, then slowly went on towards her uncle. She greatly respected that surly and taciturn man and did not manage to talk to him. Her uncle looked at her over his spectacles, put his hand on her shoulder and said: "You've grown since last year. What about school? Are you still doing well?"

Vilma made a gesture as if to say: so-so, and as she did so her mind went to an incident from her childhood. She might have been six, and she'd been made to read out an article to her uncle and aunt. She'd read something about the launching of a trans-Atlantic liner, describing the ceremony, the personalities, the emotions of the occasion, and everyone around her smiled and said: she reads like a big girl. She thought regretfully that she was no longer so careful, she'd changed, her thoughts often wandered off, and as she reflected about these things she was beset by a sense of insecurity.

Her uncle said: "One of these days I'll have a look at you, you're at a difficult age. Do you eat?"

Vilma said she did. Her uncle eyed her further: what lovely hair, then got distracted, turned towards the sea and muttered: "I want to see whether your cousin Gustavo has brought the boat back in."

He swung away from her and went off towards the pier, but went on thinking: she's pretty, is Vilma, a gentle child, or so she seems. A pity about her family. Vilma's father, years and years earlier, had gone off without any apparent reason and since then hadn't sent much news. The Professor grew gloomy in thinking of his brother and stood still until he could hear the sound of oars dipping in the water and the shape of his son's dinghy came into view.

"Did you fish?" cried the father. "Did you catch anything?"

"They aren't biting," the lad replied. "I haven't caught a thing."

He dropped anchor, lashed the boat to the iron ring and leapt ashore. He was sturdy and well-tanned and moved calmly and precisely. He came up to his father and looked at him quietly. Round them was the moon's pale light. Gustavo said: "That's the end of my fishing for this year."

"At what time are you leaving?"

"Very early tomorrow morning. We'll say goodbye now, Papa."

His father nodded and muttered: "Certainly. Will it be a long trip?"

"The usual, a couple of months; we're going via Suez to Bombay, and then round India."

They remained silent, each thinking of the coming months of separation and loneliness and his father wondering for the umpteenth time: why should he have wanted to leave? He tried to drive that thought away and told himself: everyone has his own destiny. He raised his head and, touching his son's arm, muttered: "Do look after your health." He cleared his throat and added quickly: "These are bad times. Anything might happen and we'll be so far apart."

Gustavo stared at his father in astonishment, he always said little and appeared aloof from everything. He gave him a smile and said: "What d'you expect to happen, Papa?" He lifted up his finger and said: "The wind's changed. You won't be taking the boat out tomorrow."

There was a creaking from the dinghy as it was buffeted against the pier. They carried on walking towards the house which could be made out through the pine trunks and the wind was making the lantern swing over the front door.

The Professor's eyes followed his son as he ascended the steps and he sat down on the step just below the house. The lantern illuminated the small grassy clearing, immediately beyond rose the black shapes of the pines. From the upper floor came the voices of his wife and Gustavo whispering away, her voice uppermost. The Professor shook his head and reflected once more about that son of his who was going away, he pictured to himself the ship as he had seen it the first time he saw him off, the pier crowded with people, the excitement and the women's tears. Amelia's voice had been stilled. The Professor recollected that he must make a call to see a friend of his the next day, he thought his condition gave cause for concern. "I must get to the bottom of it," he told himself, "and give him some tests." The thought of his invalid friend upset him, he got up and turned out the lantern because of the midges. As soon as he had done so, he became aware of the moonlight and couldn't help gazing up at the sky.

Vilma passed by him carrying the folded rug. Her hair fell down over her face, which looked even smaller. Her uncle reflected: "She needs to put on weight, one of these days I'll give her something, put her on a diet."

As she went by, Vilma said: "Good night, uncle Giunio."

She tip-toed into the house. She opened a wall-cupboard and left the rug there as she had been told. She looked around, the house was silent, it seemed as though no one was there. She felt relieved, her relatives made her feel uncomfortable, she had the impression she was being watched, being put to some sort of a test. Especially by aunt

Amelia, who stared at her, cross-questioned her about her wishes, her habits. At times she appeared to be on the point of saying something to her, then she'd look down and give a sigh. Vilma shrugged her shoulders, and took a couple of steps towards the great mirror between the two doors. The mirror showed her reflection: her colouring had already changed with that day in the sun and her light-coloured eyes stood out. She swept the hair back from her forehead, came closer to the mirror, examined herself, smiled at herself, felt a moment's joy and lifted up her arms. She ran out through the back door so as not to meet her uncle and slipped into the pine wood. The trees resembled a dark-uniformed detachment marching down to the sea. When she came out of the wood, the moon, already high up, was gleaming in the clear sky and high lighting the white-cliffed coast. Vilma huddled up on the ground and stayed there gazing, over-whelmed by thoughts and disquietudes, sighed and gazed.

Amelia on the upper floor crossed paths with Rita who was emerging from the child's room. She had a pair of pants in her hands and said softly: "I must wash them, they're stiff with salt."

"Right," said the grandmother. She went up to her daughter and added in agitation: "Haven't you noticed? Haven't you seen the way your father is?"

Rita avoided her gaze and answered lightly: "Go on, Mama, he's always been a ruffian."

Her mother, almost overcome by trembling, started shaking her head and returned: "He wasn't this way once. He's become aggressive, the other day he almost frightened me." And as she said this she went bright red and sweat stood out on her forehead. Rita looked at her in alarm and cried out: "Oh, I beg you, don't tell me these things." Some tears suddenly rolled down her cheeks and she embraced her mother and felt greatly comforted for a moment.

Her mother hugged her to herself, they caressed each other and her mother, holding her tight, whispered: "If I can't talk to you, who can I talk to?"

Rita nodded repeatedly.

Her mother went on more calmly: "Has anything happened that I don't know about? Or your husband perhaps?"

Rita said: "No, no." She lowered her gaze and added nothing further. It occurred to her that she'd really never succeeded in opening out fully with her mother and that maybe, if she had, things would have turned out differently. She detached herself from the embrace and said: "Nothing's happened. You know the sea gets on my nerves. And then people are saying such things."

Gustavo opened wide the shutters in his room without turning on the light. The moonlight coming through his window enabled him to move about. He gathered together the few things he needed to take with him. Whilst assembling these objects he reflected that by the same time on the following day he'd already be on the high seas, he imagined the long, uneventful voyage ahead of him. The distance he was about to travel recalled his mind to his parents and for the first time he pondered on the fact that they were no longer young. This thought troubled him. He continued to move softly across the room and seemed little more than a shadow.

Their mother abandoned herself upon the wicker couch facing out on to the verandah. The pine boughs were almost touching her, damp gusts came from the sea. She felt confused, she took her mind back to Rita's tears. Was her marriage not working? She lay there, her hands upon her lap, and she recalled the first meetings between Lino and Rita when both appeared so cheerful and secure. She told herself that since the boy had been born she had paid less attention to Rita and that had surely been a mistake. She mused that she could go and stay with them for a while, possibly in the early autumn, but she suddenly wondered whether her presence was really desired, and, in the end, searching herself, she told herself that neither did she wish to leave her house, even though it was now an empty house. Gustavo was just about to leave and would be away for a long time, but even when he was around it was hard to talk to him. Children – she thought – when they're away you long to see them, then, when they're there . . . She closed her eyes and tried to stem her thoughts. She heard Lino's voice calling: Rita, Rita, where are you? She went to the window and saw in front of the house the figure of her daughter's husband walking up and down: he'd take a few steps and stop, his hands joined behind his now stooping back, his eyes fixed on the sky. Her irritation and discontent dissolved. Some-one had put out the lantern and the magical moonlight bathed the blackness of the pine wood.

Rita rushed out of the door, crossed a narrow section of the pine wood and, reaching its edge, where the cultivated fields began, stopped. That spot, sheltered by the trees, was warmer, the earth was warm to the touch and the fragrance of ripe fruit wafted there. Rita stood motionless. She was at odds with herself, confused desires and fears weighed upon her heart, the thought occurred to her that everything could change and who knows what events might still happen.

She heard footsteps and glimpsed Lino and Vilma walk-ing through the trees; Lino, as usual, was talking and using his hands to express himself and seemed to be pointing up at the sky.

She heard her brother calling out to her from the house: "Come, Rita, the baby's crying in his sleep."

Her mother replied: "That's nothing. He often does that, like lots of children. He must have had a bad dream."

Rita moved off slowly in the moonlight. "I'm going to him," she said to herself. "If he wakes up and sees me, he'll calm down immediately."

She looked upwards and gestured into the air, entranced: light clouds drifted around the moon which disappeared, immediately reappeared, white and mysterious.

Organizing a scene

From the entrance hall there came the voices of Dado and his mother. Liana propped herself up against her pillow and mused: they'll be coming to see me. She tidied her hair, smoothed down the bedsheets and kept her eyes on the door. In the passage, her mother's and Dado's mother's voices overlapped, signora Evi's voice won through for an instant, then a door was shut and the voices could no longer be heard.

Liana let her head fall back on the pillow. The maid came in and said: "Are you feeling feverish?"

"Yes," replied Liana. She pointed to the thermometer on the bedside table. "My temperature's thirty-seven point five."

"Poor Liana," said Maria, "you still have a temperature."

Liana smiled to herself, for she wasn't a bit keen to get better, but said nothing.

"It's time for your medicine," Maria went on, uncorking a bottle.

Liana stretched forward to take the spoonful of syrup which the girl held out to her.

Dado's voice came from just outside her room.

"May I?" inquired the young man. "May I come in?"

"Do," Maria answered for her. "Do come in."

Dado opened the door and entered. He was a dark young fellow, extremely tall, and filled almost the entire doorway. On seeing him, Liana felt her heart begin to beat. She found this next-door neighbour, the son of one of her mother's friends, immensely good-looking.

"How are you, silly?" asked Dado.

The girl flushed with pleasure and replied almost inaudibly: "So-so. Not too good."

"We wanted to take you to the cinema," he said. "It would have been fun." He smiled as he looked at her: this girl had a way of moving and speaking all of her own, shy yet graceful, and he often looked at her with amused interest. The thought crossed his mind that this might possibly be his last chance to take her to the cinema, and a sound escaped him, something like a sigh, as his mind went racing across the oceans searching for a landfall to drop anchor.

Liana was asking him: "Was it going to be an Italian film or an American one?"

Dado's eyes were far away and his forehead was creased. Liana thought: he's not listening to me. I wonder what he's thinking about. She laid her head on the pillow. Suddenly feeling tired. She rubbed her hands together, as they were burning with the fever.

The young man came up to the bed, ran a finger across her forehead, as he'd occasionally done before, and said to her gently: "Do get better, or we won't be friends."

Liana sighed, reddened again and said, "Yes, yes."

Dado left the room, and she heard the sound of the voices of the two women walking down the passage to the front door.

Liana closed her eyes and pretended to be asleep. She went over the scene in her mind: she imagined that Dado was outside her room, she awaited him anew, her heart started beating as it had a few moments ago: the door opened, Dado entered, he gazed at her with his deep, dark eyes. Liana had never seen anything lovelier than those eyes. Her mind wandered away from the scene and she felt her disappointment about the cinema, if she'd been well she'd have sat between Dado and his mother to see the film. But the thought of their being that close for such a long time scared her: trapped between them, she'd have had to answer all their questions, how could she have risen to the occasion? How could she have covered up her shyness? She reddened, she wiped out the present and mused: in a year's time I'll be different. She could see the older girls at school, they talked and laughed and joined in with the boys. She hoped, willed that some day or other she would shake off the hindrance that made her different from the way she wanted to be. Once she was grown up, her awkwardness would melt away, she would move freely, she'd no longer be scared.

Maria came in again and sat at the foot of her bed.

"What are you doing?" she asked.

"Nothing."

"I bet you've a book underneath the bedclothes."

Liana smiled, nodded, and said quietly: "But don't tell mama."

Maria went round the bed arranging the bedclothes and said: "When I was at home, on winter evenings, my father used to read us the medieval romances about the kings and queens of France. I did enjoy that."

Liana looked at her with interest. She liked Maria, she was a tall, blonde girl with grey eyes, set very deep, very lively. When she had a free moment from her housework, she would come to see her and joke with her, she used to say about her father: he's huge – just imagine, his head comes out of his ears. She would tell her about life in the country, she'd looked after the cows when she was a small girl and swore they were intelligent beasts: she'd call them and they'd respond, they'd recognize her voice. Liana felt sorry that Maria worked as a housemaid and asked, in spite of herself: "Will you always do this kind of job?"

Maria seemed perturbed, then her eyes gleamed, she laughed out loud and said: "Oh, I hope not, I really hope not. I'm bound to find a husband, don't you think?"

They both laughed at the idea and Liana asked excitedly: "Who d'you like? Say, which film star do you like?"

Maria replied with a shrug, "I don't know." She gave a wink and added: "I like blonds."

"Would you like a *carabiniere*?"

They heard her mother's footsteps in the passage, exchanged glances and put on a serious expression. Maria picked up the empty glass off the bedside table, replaced the thermometer into its case. When the signora came in, she told her, "Liana's still running a temperature."

Her mother gave Liana a vexed look and retorted: "She is a tiresome child."

She went to the window and drew the curtains, then turned on the standard lamp. The room had some pretty hues – beige, white, blue – and the outlines of the furniture looked hazy on account of the lampshades. The lady stood beside the lampstand, she looked preoccupied.

"What did signora Evi have to say?"

Her mother shifted her gaze and let slip a sigh.

"Did signora Evi have something nice to tell you?" the child persisted.

"No, no. Grown-up conversation. Now let's take your temperature."

Liana reluctantly undid her nightie at the neck. Grown-up conversation interested her greatly and, besides, she was almost grown-up and capable of understanding everything. She wriggled in her bed with annoyance and went on thinking about Dado's mother, whom she liked. She was pleased when a few years earlier she and her son had come to live in the same building. She spoke Italian in a halting way that made you laugh. On some evenings she would go downstairs to their apartment and chat with her mother and she'd be allowed to stay up late. On occasion, signora Evi would talk about the country where she'd been born, on the shores of the Baltic, and it seemed that there, before the world war, everybody had led a merry, carefree life. She also told stories about the end of the war and how she'd crossed half of Europe unaccompanied and without any money. Liana removed the thermometer and said:

"Mama, I'd like to see the world."

Her mama smiled and replied, "First, though, you'll have to get better."

Maria arrived in Liana's room with her chest heaving. She was all red and her eyes were glistening. She said in a low voice:

"If you weren't here, I wouldn't stay on."

Upset, Liana looked at her and said, "Sit down a minute." She lifted up the bedclothes and continued: "I've nearly finished *The Count of Montecristo*. Whenever you like, I'll let you have it."

Maria was staring into space, her face serious. She said: "It's awful being in service, you know. It's worse than I expected."

Liana sat up in bed. She couldn't get herself to say what she was so eager to say, she couldn't even touch Maria, it wouldn't come naturally to her. She swept back her hair from her eyes and complained: "I have a headache. And I've heard something to do with signora Evi. Have you heard?"

Maria seemed to break out of her thoughts, reflected a moment and replied, "I've heard something. They're Jewish, aren't they?"

Liana nodded and avoided the other girl's gaze. She was put out by the direct question. Maria added: "There aren't any Jews in my town. I'd never seen one before."

"What's different about them, do you think?"

"I don't know. Nothing, as far as I can see. And signora Evi, poor thing, she's so kind."

"Why d'you say poor thing?"

Maria made a vague gesture and said nothing. There was the sound of footsteps, the ringing voice of aunt Betti and the more subdued voice of Liana's mother. The two women entered the room.

"Good day, Miss Betti," said Maria, and she went out.

"Oh," cried aunt Betti, "this girl's in bed again. I'd say she indulges in sloth."

Liana went red with anger, merely said *ciao* and picked up her book. The sisters engaged in close conversation and Liana engrossed herself in reading and for a while it was as though there wasn't a living soul in the room.

Suddenly, she was all attention: her aunt, leaning against the window, was speaking swiftly in a high-pitched but agreeable voice.

"I went to the cafe with Ester Salom," she was saying. "She's beside herself, just imagine – her husband Niko is planning to clear out, he simply wants to drop everything. He's terrified of what might happen, even in this country."

"Has it come to such a pass?" Liana's mother asked calmly. "God, it seems impossible, I really can't believe it."

"Exactly: Ester swears that Niko's being neurotic and that he's always been terrified of everything. She's not intending to leave, she says: I'm not moving, I couldn't live anywhere else." Aunt Betti added, "Niko will end up by going away, Ester will stay behind, so their marriage . . ." And she made a gesture as of throwing something away.

Liana knew Ester Salom well. She was her aunt Betti's

friend, a lady with a face full of freckles, large eyes and beautiful clothes. Once she'd been with her mother to see her in her apartment. She remembered the large drawing-room and her mother, admiring the glass tables and the low settees, saying: oh, it's so modern! Out of the broad windows, as they were on one of the upper storeys, she'd seen the sweep of the bay and it had impressed her. Liana connected the fact that Ester didn't want to leave with that image and would have liked to tell her aunt about it, but she knew that was a subject for grown-ups. She secretly eyed the two women and was astonished at their long faces, aunt Betti's too, though she was usually laughing and joking and pulling her leg, which greatly irritated her, so that she thought her aunt really didn't understand a thing.

"Come. Come away," said her mother. Then, turning to Liana, she said, "We'll come back so Aunt Betti can say goodbye to you."

The child made a sign with her head and said not a word. Instead she picked up a book which she'd read over and over again but which she still enjoyed. Though she knew the story almost off by heart, when she began to read it she was seized once more by a thrill of anxiety: "*I was greatly alarmed to see behind me, coming after me, the Gentleman in Grey! When he had caught up with me he doffed his hat with a bow lower than anyone had ever made to me. There was no doubt, he wished to speak to me and I could not avoid him without appearing uncouth. I too removed my hat with a bow and stood there, bare-headed in the sun, as if I were pinned to the ground. I stared at him gripped by terror, like a bird mesmerized by a snake. He too seemed greatly embarrassed. He repeated his bow without ever lifting up his eyes, came up to me and finally addressed me in a subdued and faltering voice, almost in the manner of a beggar: — The gentleman will pardon the liberty I am taking in addressing him without even knowing him*".

Maria opened the door and said cheerfully, "Liana, your friend's here."

"I've fetched your homework," said Erica. She entered the room and laid down the folder. Everything had been tidied up and the room was full of light. Liana smiled and said, as she took the copybook which her friend held out to her, "Well done, you remembered."

"When are you coming back to school?"

"I don't know," said Liana. "Soon, I think."

Erica closed the folder, took a turn around the room, stopped to look at the books on the shelf, then said: "I've been enjoying myself ever so much these days. I and Fiora never stop laughing."

"With Fiora?"

"Yes, yes," replied Erica. "We get on ever so well. We've become great friends."

Liana's mother appeared and said: "Hallo, Erica. Is there anything you'd like?"

"No thanks," said the girl, with a bob of her head. "I'm off right away, papa's waiting for me."

The signora shut the door and Erica went on: "So when are you coming back? Fiora and I have decided we're going skating. And we'll also be going to dancing school."

"Dancing school?" Liana felt bewildered by all those plans. She thought vaguely that her mother would be against dancing school, which was bound to be expensive. She cast a sceptical glance over her friend's ungainly physique and asked: "But do you like dancing?"

Erica's face clouded over, she realized it hadn't occurred to her and didn't know what to reply. She looked resentfully at her friend. So Liana said, to earn forgiveness: "Would you like to have one of my books? Or a couple?"

Erica shook her head and replied grudgingly: "Fiora's lent me a novel. A suitable one though."

Liana felt a kind of twinge, she felt out of sorts, overcome by melancholy. She raised her head and said with a faint superior smile: "I like other things. I read other things." She picked up her Latin exercise-book and added, leafing through it, "You haven't got too far ahead, luckily." And she mused: when I go back, I want to be really clever.

When Erica had gone, Liana still remained sitting up in bed, thinking. She wondered about so many things and her heart felt oppressed. Then she thought: now I'll organize a scene. She went up to the window, squeezed in behind a curtain and, as she gazed at the blue sky and the glitter of the sunshine upon the sea, decided: now I'm grown up, my friends, with their babies in their arms, come to see me, to say goodbye, because I'm going on a long journey.

Suddenly the building was full of movement. The front door had been left open so that voices and sounds reached her even from the staircase. Liana's mother was going up to the flat above, where Dado and his mother lived, or else it was the latter coming down. Early in the afternoon, Dado appeared with an old *Fräulein* who had years before taught signora Evi a bit of Italian and Liana a bit of German, had remained attached to the ladies and did little favours for them.

Liana, who was still convalescing, had to stay in her room so as not to catch a chill, but she'd got permission to leave her door ajar, so she could at least partly follow what was going on. She heard Dado's mother saying: "*Es muss sein. Man muss es machen.*"

It seemed like another voice, full of tears, perhaps. The *Fräulein* too was talking loudly, her Rs buzzing like bees. All of a sudden she cried: "*Ich schäme mich, ich schäme mich für mein Land.*"

Dado's mother began again in Italian, drawing out her words in a sing-song. When she was speaking Italian she'd wrestle with verb-tenses and verb-endings and would finally say: "Always continues my war with your language."

Liana smiled to herself, got up and went over to the light-coloured shelf that ran along the wall and held her books. She looked at them and ran through their titles again, and reading them, as always, gave her a profound pleasure.

Maria hurried into the room, opened the wardrobe and began to search for something. Liana's mother called her: "Come here. We need you."

The *Fräulein* appeared at the door for an instant, gave Liana a smile and said: "You've grown taller. Fever makes you grow, *weiss du*?"

Liana said "yes" happily and looked at herself in the mirror over the chest-of-drawers. Her arms were long and her slender body was undergoing a change. Her skin was pink and her chestnut hair fell almost as far as her shoulders: she contemplated herself, smiled, looked serious and was alternately pleased and not pleased with herself.

Dado had entered the room and was standing still. When Liana noticed him, she blushed and felt hot all over, then said in a low voice, "D'you know, I've grown."

She glanced at her friend again and saw he was wearing his shirt open, showing his powerful neck, and his curly dark hair was dishevelled. She was amazed to see him looking so different from usual, but was overcome by shyness, lowered her eyes and said nothing.

Dado drew near to the child and asked, "How old are you?"

"Eleven. In two months' time."

A rueful expression came over the lad's face, and he said: "A pity, I won't be around for your birthday."

Liana had sensed the something was afoot, still she asked: "Why?"

"We're going away," replied the lad. "Leaving."

"Soon?"

Dado nodded. He glanced around him: the room was full of light and from the two large windows could be seen a strip of sea and the seaplane base. He said quietly: "Who knows whether we shall meet again some day."

"Dado," called the *Fräulein* from the passage, "you must be quick."

Maria came in and said: "The removal men will be here soon. Your mother says you're to come away."

The young man looked grave and Liana thought that unkempt as he was and with a growing beard he looked older than his twenty years, but that he was very good-looking just the same.

Dado held out to the girl a tiny suitcase of dark crocodile-skin and said: "Here's a present for you. You'll find two or three little things inside it." A shaft of sunlight lit up the room, and the young man following it, thought that he would never forget that blue and gilt town and his departure – this leave-taking – seemed to him unreal. He came up to the child, kissed her fine hair and repeated: "*Ciao*, Liana. Keep up to the mark."

Signora Evi walked briskly in and also embraced her. "Here, this is my dress handbag. Viennese *petit point*. It's a keepsake from me, it's yours. Oh, you are pretty!" she cried, and rushed out.

Soon silence took over the apartment. Liana's mother had gone out. Maria had shut herself in the kitchen to wash the dishes. Liana slowly undressed, picked up her book and slid under the bedclothes. Her bedside light lit up her pillow and a small section of the room, the blue rug and the picture of the little dogs. The girl opened her book and started reading, but she couldn't concentrate and her mind strayed this way and that.

She woke up to find Maria drawing open the curtains and immediately said to her: "I've had a dream. Listen well, I want to tell you it. I was there, on the rug, I was looking towards the door when suddenly it opens wide and a whole procession of people starts to pour into the room: grown-ups and children and even animals with luminous eyes, horrible! They're all staring at me, the grown-ups laugh, and some of them shake their fist menacingly. As the procession continues to file in, voices are heard crying out: Watch out! There's a huge devil after us." Liana heaved a long breath and said: "It gave me such a fright that I woke up with a start."

Maria put her hand on her shoulder and replied: "Oh, dreams, people do get some strange ones. Don't think about it any more."

"It was horrible, even the colours were horrible, greens and blacks."

"At my home we were always telling each other our dreams and my mother used to send me, in secret, to put money on the numbers in the lottery."

Maria seemed to be following her own train of thought

and as she tied up her apron she was smiling.

Liana swallowed hard a few times, felt her throat and said: "I think I have a temperature again."

The girl laid her hand on Liana's forehead and answered: "In that case I'll go and call your mama."

Liana stretched full length in bed: she hoped she did have a temperature. She mused that she didn't feel like going to school; then straight away, remembering her class-mates, she reflected that she did like it really, there were lots of things that interested her and she was happy to be among her friends, their tales roused her curiosity, she had a good time with them, she laughed, but she felt she was having a life quite different from her home life and it sometimes made her suffer. Maybe that was why she wished she had a temperature.

She swallowed two or three times and it hurt, but not too badly. She heard Maria's voice asking her mother what she was to prepare for breakfast. After a while she heard her mother making a telephone call, perhaps she was asking the doctor for the day's instructions. She shut her eyes and the hustle and bustle of the evening before came back to her. With her heart beating faster, she organized a scene: Dado stood before her, gazing at her with that deep look of his and saying, "How are you, silly?" She reflected that the young man was leaving, who knows when she'd see him again and straight away she organized another scene: she had now become a young lady, she was there in her own room, she knew that Dado had disembarked from the ship and was making his way down the waterfront towards his old house. She could see his barely changed face and his different stride. There, Dado was at the door, he was ringing the bell. Liana got out of her bed and took a step towards the door. She tried to imagine the meeting, she pictured the young man's amazement at seeing her so grown-up and beautiful, naturally. She searched for the words she would address to him, but found it difficult. So she picked up the little crocodile-skin suitcase and took out the carved wooden objects that Dado had put inside it for her – a little hunchback with his hands in his pockets, a young hare on skis and a Chinaman with a rickshaw. She'd seen them so many times on the mantel piece in Dado's room; he would laugh as he looked at them and he'd say: one day I'll give them to you. She set them up on her bedside table and found they looked lovely, she would have liked to show them to Erica and her other friends, but she then considered that they wouldn't understand how extraordinary they were. She decided not to show them to anybody or to say a word about how she'd come by them.

The dining-room clock struck. Maria came back in and said: "Your mama says you're to get dressed."

"Yes, yes," said the child, and she was almost pleased she had to do it.

"Here's your skirt," Maria went on. She came up to her and added: "I've had a strange dream too, would you like to hear it?"

Liana nodded and Maria recounted: "I could see a great deal of sea and you could tell that now it was going to drown all the land. There was no escape, the waves were beginning to rise and people were already beginning to die a watery death. But all of a sudden I could make out a bright light on the horizon, like you see before the sun rises, and from that bright light I gathered that the sea was retreating and the world could start living again."

Absorbed, Liana said: "That was a frightening dream."

"It was at first. Afterwards, though, I was happy, there was that beautiful light and we all knew that the danger was over."

The doorbell rang and Liana's mother called Maria. Liana heard the girl's hurried footsteps, mingled voices, and the clink of the milkwoman's containers as she went into the kitchen and dispensed milk in her zinc measuring-bowl. Liana sat down on her bed again and contemplated the outline of the window and the pale early morning sky. She thought perhaps today she'd gladly go to school, she'd been away too long.

Maria came back and reported: "It was the milk. Well, are

you getting dressed?"

The child turned round, looked at the girl and asked: "Have you worked out where Dado and signora Evi are going?"

Maria nodded.

"Well, then?"

Maria picked up the comb and went over to the child. She said: "I've heard them say so many things. Ester Salom's husband is going, too. Your aunt Betti was telling the *Fräulein* about it yesterday."

Liana thought for a moment of Ester's apartment, of her husband, shook her head and asked again: "But where are Dado and his mother off to? Is it far?"

Maria began to comb the little girl's hair and replied: "I think they're going to America. The *Fräulein* told me the secret. She's against it, she says it's crazy to dash off like that, without any plans, without asking anybody's advice. She kept saying: you just don't go off like that, a single woman with a son who hasn't completed his studies. What will she do, poor Evi? How will they get by in such a huge, unknown country?"

She arranged her apron and added, poor things.

Liana wanted to retort: Don't say poor things, but she said nothing. When Maria had gone, she picked up her wooden figures again and put them in the suitcase. She grasped the suitcase by the handle, like a traveller, and began walking up and down the room. She wanted to organize a scene: in front of her she could see the dark-coloured sea, the huge, unknown country, her friends departing, she was grown-up, she was weeping and crying: goodbye, farewell for ever.

The new home

The car advanced slowly. Along the nearly dark track, the Trevis made out the villa they thought they had to go to.

"There's the house, I think I remember it," said signor Trevi to the driver. "You know, Lina, this must be it."

When they got out and her husband paused a moment to pay the fare, signora Trevi saw someone coming towards them, a massive figure with a withdrawn expression.

"Is that where you're going?" he asked, and raised his arm towards the house. "Is that where you're going? Is it your car?"

"I'm Guido Trevi," replied the man. "We came by taxi, it was easier."

The man gave him a surprised look but immediately replied: "Trevi? After you, please. That way."

Signor Trevi stepped forward uncertainly and mused: yet something has changed, it doesn't look the same. And he looked around shaking his head.

They walked a stretch in the dark, then went along a driveway, umbrella pines and dark shrubs flanking both sides. The villa entrance was moderately well lit, its heavy, low door and sloping porch roof could be made out.

When they went into the entrance hall, there was nobody there, the man who had shown them the way, hearing the sound of an engine, had rushed out again, the house was silent and signora Trevi thought it felt uninhabited.

The end door opened, and the lady of the house came towards them her smile restrained, her small jacket glittering like a breast-plate.

"Good evening," she cried, holding out her hand, "good evening. Here we are in our new home." She glanced at the couple somewhat anxiously and added: "You knew it well before."

Signora Trevi shook her head and said at once: "Oh, no. It

was only my husband that used to come here to visit Fazio."

The gentleman of the house had now also appeared. Signor Trevi addressed him also, saying: "I used to come here often, but so many years have gone by. I used to come here in the seventies, up to perhaps 1975." He stopped and looked around, then asked: "With whom did you negotiate the purchase?"

"The first time we came to see the house, Leo was still here. Fazio had been dead a few months. It was Leo who showed us round the house and grounds. But he wouldn't negotiate, he said: discuss it with my lawyer. By the end of our visit he was very pale, agitated."

Their host had said all this lightly. His dog-like face had broadened into a smile and seemed to be saying: that's life, everything changes.

Voices were heard and at once signor Bai appeared and handed the butler a bundle wrapped in white cloth. He laughed, and so did their hostess.

"Ah," said Bai, "I won't break my diet, but that doesn't make me give up my friends either."

The butler crossed the room carrying the tray wrapped in the white serviette.

"Everything's there," Bai went on. "You'll see, I'm not depriving myself of anything, but it's all been strained and de-fatted."

Signora Bai came in, having paused in front of the mirror. She was a tall blonde woman. She moved forward balancing on her silver stiletto heels, straight as a sergeant-at-arms. At every step she took, her long legs showed through the slit down her skirt.

"Here we are," she said with pleasure, "here we all are together again after the summer."

Signora Trevi took a seat, observed her husband's uneasy air and eventually remarked: "Haven't you knocked down a wall or two?" And she waved her hand at the altered spaces.

Their hostess, with creased eyebrows, returned: "There were three small rooms here on the ground floor. Everything looked smaller, I don't know how they managed."

"Perhaps they found it more convenient," interjected her husband. "There was even a partition over there, maybe one of them would rehearse on one side and one on the other."

"Yes, of course," said Trevi, as if talking to himself. "That's where the partition was, and over there the display board with stage photographs."

"We saw Fazio on stage just a few days before he died. It was a Sunday afternoon and at the end he scored a great personal success."

Lina Trevi fell silent. She had the impression that the others weren't interested in that topic. She leaned back against her armchair and sat listening to what the others were saying but realized she was going along with them without listening. Something was distracting her, her brain felt muffled and so she pulled herself up sharply as if she wanted to shake off some malaise.

"Are you cold?" her husband asked kindly. "Are you all right?"

She smiled and replied quietly: "I was thinking. About him."

Signor Trevi went slightly pale and said: "I don't want to think about it. It happened so suddenly. And now Leo's dead, too." He made a gesture of dismay and moved away from his wife.

Some guests arrived. Angela stepped daintily forward, slightly askew, as if trying to avoid her large bosom being noticed. She began smilingly greeting her friends.

Signor Trevi said to their host: "You have some splendid paintings. Nineteenth-century Lombard, I think?"

"Yes," the man replied. "I started collecting them when no one wanted them and got them for a song."

"Aren't you afraid of burglars?" asked Angela. "Do you feel safe?" A shadow crossed her eyes and she added: "I wouldn't."

Their host nodded towards the man who was walking to and fro between the villa and the garden with swift, elastic strides, and murmured: "In fact, that fellow there says I ought to get a shot-gun, he's very insistent, but I don't like the idea." He chuckled and added: "Weapons to him are what our hands are to us."

"What did he do before?" asked signora Trevi. "Where did you find him?"

But the butler had approached to put out a torch that was guttering and smoking just outside the front door, and the conversation ended. Their hostess filled in the gap by relating a story of her childhood. As she spoke she barely moved her head, which she held erect, and as she had high cheek-bones and dark, taut skin, she looked like an idol. Her large eyes sparkled.

The serving-maid brought in a very elaborate dish coloured pink and orange and nobody could make out what it was made of.

Guido Trevi said: "Easy: we're eating colours."

All concurred, even signora Trevi smiled, without joining in the conversation. She couldn't deflect her thoughts. She struggled with them several times, as she had been doing frequently of late, but her thoughts were more powerful than she, they presented themselves, fixed and bright, and she could not dislodge them. This thought – this image – was: Fazio in his changing room and she could see the dazzling light above the mirror and the jumble of costumes. On that Sunday afternoon she had been loth to go back-stage, but Fazio had embraced them, the artificial tone which she'd known him to have for years was quite gone, he spoke to them warmly. When the lad entered who was his partner in the play, the two actors had smiled at each other, the senior quipped away with the junior and appeared to yield himself up to the other with every glance. The scene was intense, breathing love.

As they left the theatre, in the night, they'd gone on talking and someone had kept on saying: Fazio has a superb moment.

Lina Trevi got up, crossed the dining-room with her hesitant step, and sat next to Nora Bai. Trevi also sat down next to the two women and said rapidly: "Do you remember how outstanding Fazio was? I followed him from the very beginning, he was then a literature student, yet it was as though he'd never done anything else in his life but act. I wonder what his greatest quality was?"

He bent his head and said no more. The maid came round with the coffee-tray with jug and cups. Their hostess said: "My friend Bardi promised to come. He's always so busy."

Nora Bai said: "Oh, I would like to see him, I do find his conversation amusing."

There was a furious barking of dogs, they seemed to be calling one another and just wouldn't stop. The guests pricked up their ears for a moment. Nora asked: "What about your Wolf? Where's your dog?"

"He's at school," replied their hostess. "I've sent him off to school."

"He's got to be taught how to defend himself and how to attack," answered their host. He sighed: "A pity. He was such an affectionate animal, sometimes I found him really touching." And he smiled as he thought of his dog.

Their hostess invited them all out under the porch at the front of the house. Torches illuminated the English lawn and the little bowling green beyond it. Guido Trevi took a few steps over the lawn. The grass, under that uncertain glow, took on a curious, stagey yellow-green colour. The guests' voices sounded fainter now, and he felt relieved. He stopped in the middle of the lawn and drew a long breath. He could see Fazio on stage, close to the wings, he could see his pale face, his sharp gaze, and across that great gulf he caught the echo of one of his lines: *More time will go by and the entire present will appear as something hostile, burdensome . . .* How many years had gone by since that performance? How many? He couldn't remember, he absolutely had to work it out, he wanted to fix it forever in his memory, he wanted it not to be swallowed up in the confused, indistinct whirl of the past. He gestured vaguely and reflected that that had been a different epoch, friendship and projects blossomed and everybody seemed to move on a steady platform, not an inclined plane.

There were voices, some of the guests joined him on the lawn. Along the sides, at a distance, great cedars towered upwards, forming the wings. They strolled along in silence, like shadows, only their host said: "What a lovely night. You wouldn't think summer was over."

Their group were heading for the gazebo, a little nineteenth-century temple which stood alongside the boundary wall and had a newly restored frieze. A wrought-iron lantern lit up the place. There was a rustling sound and Angela cried out: something touched me. She put her hands to her hair and her great bosom was heaving. Everybody stood still and Trevi said: "It must have been a bat. They seem to come straight at you, but their radar keeps them clear of everything."

There was more rustling, but it wasn't clear where it came from, it might have been the wind teasing the tops of the tall trees. They all looked up at the sky, they could see the stars which had now turned faint.

Their host took Angela's arm and confided: "When I bought this house, someone said to me: What? Do you want to live in a place where such a terrible thing happened? And I answered: terrible things go on everywhere, only we don't know them."

Angela nodded repeatedly and sighed.

Her friend drew her further away, leaving the group. He turned to look at the villa which was illuminated from below and seemed from that distance like a little house with walls made of paper. He said: "I don't regret having come here. Yet I think – don't misunderstand me – I think I've occasionally sensed his presence." He smiled and added gently: "But, who knows, that may be no bad thing."

Angela said, a trifle ruefully: "I didn't know him, I'd only seen him on stage."

When they got back to the porch they found that the late-comers had arrived.

"Come along," cried their hostess, "come along: Bardi and Raul are here. Bardi is recounting a dream."

Bardi raised his large pale eyes and greeted them with a courtly wave of the hand. Behind him, young Raul, round-headed and slender-chested, smiled as he smoked. Bardi waited a moment for the guests to settle down, then carried on: "Oh, it's nothing, I was saying that certain elements recur frequently in my dreams. For instance: I'm crossing an Italian landscape, say of the Paolo Uccello variety, and I have to reach a fortress which is outlined against the clear sky. The fortress is close by, I can see it, yet I know I'll have to go a long way to get there. There's no one around. And another element: there's no one around but I'm aware that lots of people, including some I know in real life, are hiding somewhere and following me, perhaps benevolently and perhaps not. I can't tell, and this causes me great axiety." He took a deep breath and at last added: "When I wake up I spend a long time brooding about my dream and its symbols."

His friends appeared to be reflecting, some of them nodded. Raul got up, lit himself a cigarette and smiled at the Trevis. Lina said to him in admiration: "I know you dance well. I've been told that."

The young man replied calmly: "I'm still training, but dancing is everything to me."

Bardi intervened: "Yes, he's brilliant, his teacher says the same."

Raul resumed his seat and moved his head in little jerks, like a bird. Nora Bai took up the thread of the conversation again and said: "You know, Bardi? I don't understand the mood of your dream. And do you think there are such things as prophetic dreams?"

Someone chuckled and said quietly: "I never remember my dreams."

Lina Trevi shifted her gaze away from Raul, who captured her attention and at the same time made her feel uncomfortable. She looked round for her husband, but he had his back to the company and was contemplating the lawn. Angela, too, was standing apart, wrapped in her shawl, she looked beautiful framed in its black outline. Lina moved off towards her. She felt the silk with her fingers and said: "This is really old, isn't it?"

Angela nodded: yes, yes. She sighed, and went on: "I like being wrapped up, it makes me feel safe."

"How are you getting on?" signora Trevi asked further. "And what about your work?"

Angela smiled with pleasure and replied: "Quite well. There are quite a lot of us, you know."

"Do you get many patients?"

"They're not patients, we form a group and I try to help them sort out problems."

Nora Bai's and Bardi's voices grew loud. The woman was seated stiffly in her armchair, the lantern lit up her face and her pale arms that sliced the air with peremptory gestures. Bardi was speaking loudly too, and his sharp voice cut through the others. Raul listened, blinked repeatedly, then gave a shake of his shoulders and murmured: "God, what a conversation," and started laughing.

Others tried to intervene, signor Bai asked his wife to desist and their hostess declared: "I'm with Bardi. I always agree with him."

Bardi stood up and kissed her hand and they both laughed.

Lina Trevi looked towards the garden: some of the torches had gone out and the man who had ushered them to the house was checking the flames. A strip of the lawn was picked out by the reddish glow. Her husband had once, on his return from a visit to this house, given her a detailed account of how they had spent the day: there was Fazio's elderly mother, the actresses were there, and, of course, Leo; the garden was full of flowers, white roses especially, they had talked theatre and at the end Fazio had asked: why is Lina not with us?

Lina shrugged her shoulders. What was she doing in those days? She felt she was viewing the past across an enormous distance. What was she doing? She could see her then home, between the school and the park, Fazio, a young man, arriving with a great bouquet of carnations. She smiled at the memory of Fazio holding those flowers and was saddened to think he was dead. She stood there, her clasped hands hanging down.

"What is it?" enquired signor Bai. He stood facing her, eyeing her curiously. "What's up?"

"Nothing," Lina answered slowly. "Nothing at all." She ran her hand through her hair and continued: "Perhaps I'm a little tired."

She strolled a little way and sat down next to Angela. Bardi had fallen silent. Raul, beside him, was leaning on his armchair with a smile. Lina caught his eye, forced herself to speak, and asked him: "Well, Raul, will we be seeing you on the stage soon?"

"Oh, no," said the young man. "I'm still learning, I haven't yet got the training I want."

"What a splendid thing," said Guido Trevi. "How splendid to train for the stage." He drew close to Bardi and went on: "Don't you agree? It's a life . . ." and as he hunted for the word his face grew animated. He gestured towards the house and garden and, looking Bardi in the eye, asked in a low voice: "Did you know this house before?"

Bardi's eyes signalled in the affirmative, but his attention wandered off towards Raul.

Lina turned to her companion, she couldn't help admiring her fragile white profile, and said: "You said you work hard. And do you obtain results?"

"I work three hours a day. I couldn't keep it up for longer." Angela gave a toss of her head and her shawl slipped off. She seemed to reflect, then said, weighing her words: "Do I obtain results? Sometimes I do and sometimes I don't. But I myself have derived great benefit from it."

Lina contemplated her pensively. She took a hasty breath and couldn't help asking: "Were you in such a bad way?"

"Yes, oh, yes." The woman held up the shawl against her bosom. Her face was still, some freckles showed through her clear skin. Looking towards the garden, she replied: "I wasn't eating at all. I couldn't stop weeping. Just imagine, I'd wake up at night to find myself soaking wet. My face, my neck, my hands. And it was my own tears that had reduced me to that state, soaking wet."

Signora Trevi made a little gesture at Angela and touched her on the arm. The words died on her lips and she remained silent. An extremely bright central light had been turned on. Some of the guests had risen to take their leave, their host and hostess drew closer together, their butler strode swiftly to and fro between the villa and the front gate like a sentinel.

Nigeria

The doctor bent down, fished a map out of his bag and silently spread it out on the table, underneath the lamp. It was a 1:500,000 scale map of Nigeria. He ran his finger along a jagged line, glanced at those present and something, a kind of excitement, glinted in his eyes. With a faint smile, he said: "D'you see?" Pointing again with his finger, he went on: "This is the northern border and this is the great bend in the river."

He pointed to a small rectangle which he had marked out in ink and continued: "This is where we are. It's Sahel country with extreme variations of temperature, it's very hot during the day and at night we wrap ourselves up the way you do here up in the mountains."

He removed his hand from the map, which rolled up again instantly, took another one out of the same bag and spread that out. It was a map he'd coloured himself: a sandy pink for the land and a pretty sky-blue colour for the bodies of water. His friends, contemplating the map, exclaimed: "Isn't it lovely, you're so clever."

This time the doctor followed with his fore-finger the line where land and water met and said after a pause: "This is where our firm is building the dam. It will be eight kilometres across and will create a reservoir of water to serve the entire region."

He smiled with satisfaction, his eyes lengthened sideways behind his spectacles and a youthful expression returned to his face. He glanced at his guests and added: "I don't know when the work will be complete, you can't predict the end of a job like this. A few weeks ago it looked as if we'd made great strides, everybody in the camp was excited, then something went wrong in the building of the embankment and the river flattened the whole lot."

He looked once more at the map, sighed and repeated:

"Yes, the river flattened the whole lot and the firm began all over again. But it was all budgeted for."

A sweeping gesture across the map denoted a huge area, and he explained: "When the work is complete, this entire area will be flooded and the inhabitants, about thirty thousand in number, will have to leave their land and move elsewhere."

A thought crossed his mind, and he fell to laughing heartily. He said: "But the blacks aren't bothered. On the contrary, they go ahead happily building their houses as if there were an eternity ahead of them. That's the way they are."

The lady of the house also laughed and exclaimed: but how on earth? She got up slowly and went over to the open-plan kitchen. She brought back a tart and said: "It's made with bilberries. I know you like it, but I didn't make it."

The doctor's wife smiled with her sly little eyes, wriggled on her seat and said: "My dears, I'm longing to be off now. I hope my papers are in order at last. I've been waiting for so many months and I'm on tenterhooks."

Their host glanced now at one and now at the other of his guests with an attentive and affectionate expression and asked: "But how do people live out there? And how do they stand financially – the workers, I mean, of course?"

The doctor nodded his understanding, put away his maps and began to explain: "Everything they earn is paid to them at home. On site, they spend only pocket money. I know people who, after working for twenty or thirty months, go back home and fritter away the whole of their small fortune. Some workers traipse round the world in this fashion and occasionally meet up somewhere or other. Once I had to wait for a plane in the company of a labourer, we had to wait for hours, but my companion continually recognized friends of his among the crowd, they'd call out to each other, exchange news: where are you working? what are you doing? And they'd embrace each other joyfully. I was very struck."

He was silent for a moment and the smile died away on his lips. He shrugged, and added: "My situation is different: for the time being my pay goes to support our children over here."

His wife looked tender and cross at the same time. She held out her hand to her husband but cut the gesture short, so that her hand fell on to the table. She said quietly: "Our youngest son might come with us. It seems they're managing this year to set up some high school classes there, in which case the boy can join us."

The lady of the house nodded and enquired: "In the meantime, are you going out alone?"

"Yes," replied the woman, and bowed her head.

Their hostess had divided the tart and handed everyone a dessert plate. Her husband got to his feet, took a bottle off the dresser and examined it against the light.

"This is a *vin santo* dessert wine," he said, "made by a friend of mine." And he smiled with satisfaction as he poured it into their glasses.

The doctor started on the tart and said: "Certainly, we never see a tart like this out there." He turned to his wife and said: "If we don't have the children with us, we'll have our meals at the canteen. It's very handy."

She nodded and answered: "Of course, but you'll see: I'll get myself organized." She looked at her friend and told her: "I'm interested in the local dishes. I really want to see how they use palm oil and millet there."

Their host bent forward and asked curiously: "What about the blacks? What are the blacks like these days?"

The doctor pursed his lips, leaned back in his seat and said: "They're often very uneducated. They eat the wrong things. And they bring their children to me when there's no longer anything that can be done to save them. At first I was very upset by the deaths among infants."

There was a brief lull in the conversation. For a moment no one felt inclined to talk and an aura of faraway places seemed to hover round the hospitably arrayed table.

"Dear God," sighed their hostess. And, despite herself, her gaze lingered fondly and uneasily on her fine living-room where the light glowed warmly on the wood-panelling.

She shook herself, stood up and said to her friend: "Come, I have something to show you. It's for you." She picked up her knitting which was lying on an armchair and went on: "Lift up your arm, will you?"

She spaced out the stitches along the needles and measured the work done across her friend's chest. She stretched out the knitting slightly and said: "It's all right, isn't it?"

"It's really lovely," said the woman smoothing out the wool against her body. "Woodland colours. Thank you."

The lady of the house smiled and continued: "It will remind you of these parts."

The doctor's wife said: yes, of course. She put her arm around her friend and said with a hug: "It's the waiting that's a strain, you know. When I'm over there with my husband, it will be different. I'll feel better."

They heard the dog barking and the sharp sound of the front door shutting, then the sound of steps coming up the wooden stairs and their hosts' daughter appeared. She was very young, her face fair-skinned and her eyes full of laughter. Her chestnut hair was loosely done up in a chignon.

"What a transformation," exclaimed the doctor. "How you've changed, you've grown up."

A shadow seemed to flit through his eyes as the girl laughed and embraced her mother's friend while her parents looked on.

The doctor's wife tugged her arm and whispered something in her ear, the girl shook her head and protested, still laughingly: no, nothing of the sort, it's all nonsense. She turned to her mother and said: "If you knew how we laughed this evening. The headmaster's son turned up to the party dressed as a Spanish dancer. He's so crazy. He even did an act."

She glanced at the adults, who seemed engrossed, and repeated: how we laughed. She raised her hand to her hair and let it fall around her shoulders, so that she now looked more child-like. She looked round and said: I'm tired, terribly tired.

"Off you go," her mother said. "Go off to sleep, you have school tomorrow."

The girl embraced them all and went off to her bedroom. The doctor waited a little, then said: "She's lovely. She's become really lovely." He searched in his pockets, brought out a cornelian, displayed it in the light so that the stone appeared gilded. The doctor held it out to his hostess and said: "This is for you. A keepsake."

The woman blushed and a dark wave seemed to travel over her handsome face right down to her neck.

"Thank you," she said in a neutral voice. "Thank you." And she turned it round in her fingers, admiring it.

The doctor moved his chair up to the lady's and murmured something which the others could not catch. The other man was about to say something, but noticed that his wife's mind was on something else, her eyes were on the doctor, they had a faraway look; he stood up, cleared his throat and said loudly: "Who knows, I might come and see you this year. What d'you say, perhaps I'll get round to making the trip."

The doctor's wife clapped her hands gently and said: "That would be splendid, but I don't believe you."

There was a silence. The doctor was gazing at the other woman and slowly shaking his head. He murmured: "You'd enjoy it."

Their hostess stood up and removed the large dish with the tart and the sweet-dishes from the table. Her face with its fine and perfect features kept disappearing and reappearing.

When she'd finished, she took a seat next to the doctor's wife.

Their host caught his wife's eyes and continued: "We really must change our life-style, don't you think? We must make a move at last."

The doctor had taken a couple of walnuts and said, as he tried to crack them open: "Yes, yes, you must both come over. It's an experience. Out there I and my fellow doctor or my engineering colleagues often discuss the choice we've made and ask ourselves: what *is* this African malady? We have long discussions about it in the evenings, in the club, or after seeing a film, as we return home swathed in plaids. We ask ourselves: why are we here? We look at the heavy sky, the outlines of the prefabricated buildings and someone or other suggests an answer: it's because we want freedom, he'll say, or because one's responsibilities are greater here. I don't know."

"What have your children got to say?" the lady of the house quietly asked her friend. "Will they get by on their own?"

"Let's not talk about that now," the other woman murmured. "It hasn't been an easy decision, it's been tough for me. But my husband couldn't carry on, things were driving him mad over here."

Her friend nodded repeatedly. She gave a gentle sigh and

said in her dead voice: "Yes, I do know about these things. My son's got problems, too, he absolutely refuses to carry on with his studies."

"And what about you? What do you do about it?"

"I talk to him, I try to get him to reason things out, but he won't listen. I don't know what's going on inside him."

Her husband, who was attentively following what she said, brought his foot down to the floor and ran his hand a couple of times through his thick wavy hair. He looked annoyed and said quickly: "Do stop complaining about your son. He's a good lad, really. But you have no patience."

His wife turned pale. She shook her head and retorted: "Good? I don't know, I'm not sure. He's so superficial."

"I can't bear to listen," returned her husband, raising his voice. "I can't bear to listen to you when you talk like that."

Their guests lowered their heads. The doctor removed his glasses and said, weighing his words: "Come, come, you've got to have faith. Though sometimes it is difficult."

His wife nodded her agreement a few times and smiled at him. Their host looked at them hard, his pale eyes seemed larger and a kind of sudden astonishment flickered within them. Suppressing his disquiet, he said: "It was on account of them that we moved away from the town, so as to give them a better environment. Now things have changed, of course. Who would have imagined? Who knows, we might even leave the country."

A flash of lightning showed through the window, then followed the crash of thunder and the lights went out. The dog, under the staircase, whined.

"Stupid beast," muttered their host. "He's still scared of thunder."

He got up, picked up a candle-stick from the mantel piece nearby, lit the candle and stood it in the centre of the table. The candle flame cast a warm glimmer over the table-cloth while tall shadows leapt up the white walls.

"This is a nice house you've got," sighed the doctor. "And now you're thinking of leaving it. Are you really thinking of doing that?"

The mistress of the house pursed her lips and said quietly: "I don't know, I don't know. It's all got to be gone over." She turned to the other woman, her face looked more childlike, even her voice had changed. She confessed slowly: "For some time now I've been thinking about the future in a way that almost frightens me. I feel we can't be sure about anything, anything at all."

The doctor picked up the bottle of grappa, poured himself a good tot, and drained it at one gulp. He looked affectionately at the objects that surrounded him, then at his friends' faces and his small, lively eyes glittered in that strange light. He said in a low voice, as if meditating to himself: "The blacks in my area are Muslims. Even the skilled workers are Muslims and don't take alcohol. So they get no cirrhosis of the liver and no ulcers either, because they have no anxieties. But they have so many other diseases. Their women are often extremely beautiful. Sometimes we look at them: they go around near their houses, they wear silver bands round their foreheads. When we approach them to get a closer look they vanish silently, they slip inside their houses or wherever, but they are no longer to be seen and we exchange looks of amazement and we end up wondering: were they alive? Were they real?"

Geography of life

They came shyly up to her, but smiling, and Giulio said: "Here we are. This is Mary."

And the protective gesture which he directed towards his companion contrasted with the youthfulness of his entire person and expression.

"I'm Mary," repeated the girl in Italian with a strong American accent. She held out her hand and smiled, displaying tiny teeth, and she gave a little laugh, shrill and high-pitched like that of many English-speaking women.

Signora Elsa drew them towards her in an embrace. She had a good look at them, first the young man, whom she'd seen as a child – he was the son of a distant relation of hers by marriage – and had not had an opportunity to see again for many years.

So she looked at Giulio who looked at her in turn, heartened and smiling. She said: "Come in. I'm so pleased to see you."

The bride came past her and Elsa observed that her figure was fairly heavy and didn't match her face, which was rather long and lean. She's not good-looking – she mused – not good-looking at all. She glanced again at the lad and thought: he has his mother's eyes, dark, gentle and opaque, and almost ochre-coloured eyeballs. And in her mind she could see his mother tossing back her thick chestnut-coloured hair, laughing and gesticulating as she explained: there's Turkish blood in my veins, truly there is, I'm serious, and my father was so tough and strong. Once in a forest in Croatia he came across a bear and killed it, honest.

"But can we believe her?" Elsa used to ask, highly entertained. "Can we believe her?"

And someone or other would say: yes, yes, of course, down in that stretch of Dalmatia there was such a jumble of races."

Elsa looked at the lad once more and felt something, a small movement within herself, and realized that tears were suddenly bathing her face and she could no longer hide them. She shook her head, murmuring: "I am stupid. I'm so stupid."

She stood up and hurried out of the living-room, half laughing and half drying her eyes. She went and fetched the handkerchief out of her handbag and images from long ago flashed like film stills before her eyes: herself and the children beside a little lake, hardly more than a pond, and someone, perhaps their grandfather, had taken a picture of that day's outing: she could hear the voice of Giulio, then still a child, the drawl in which he'd nag to have something, and herself, Elsa, peacefully looking on at the children and contemplating that cherished landscape with the bright sunshine slanting down and the horizon broad and open and very gently rolling.

She returned to the living-room. The bride shifted nervously on her armchair and spread out her skirt, possibly because of the great heat or else so as not to crease it, and so it looked even more voluminous.

"It's nice here," she said. "Very nice," she repeated in English. And she looked around, shy but curious. She relaxed, reclining back in the armchair, something like relief going through her steady grey eyes. She joined her hands together on her lap and said again in English: "Very comfortable, so many books."

Her young husband, breathing that's better, that's better, looked at her fondly and said: "We've had a strenuous journey. From the campus to New York. At New York a strike made us miss our flight so that we were late arriving in Paris, where Mary has contacts for her music research. Now we're here and tomorrow we'll be in Sicily for my scientific conference." He too reclined in his armchair, let out a little sight and added: "After the conference we get to my parents at last."

Elsa smiled. Mary blinked and said hastily: "They don't know me yet. Just think, we've only spoken over the phone."

The young man gave a confirmatory nod and explained, himself astonished at the turn of events: "Last year, when my parents came to visit me, I didn't yet know Mary.

139

Everything happened so quickly between us." He held out his hand to his wife and there was an instant of smiling emotion between them. Then Giulio appeared to recollect something important, picked up his travelling-bag and said: "Look: here are our wedding photographs. I'll show them to you."

He fanned out four or five photographs and they all moved closer together so as to see them better.

"That's my campus," explained Giulio. "And that's us at home on our wedding day."

The pictures showed a square interior with bare, bright walls, a long sideboard, the table with a lace cloth, the wedding cake and the young couple standing close together.

Signora Elsa nodded again and again and murmured: very sweet, lovely.

She ran into the kitchen to fetch a bottle of champagne, her heart was beating, she thought: these young people, these marriages; but she brushed aside her further reflection and said to herself: Giulio's mother will be pleased to hear they've been here.

She returned with a smile on her face and said merrily: "We must drink a toast."

Giulio got to grips with the bottle carefully, Elsa brought the glasses, the cork shot out with a quiet pop and Mary, raising her glass, said: "Here's to you, Elsa, to the two of us."

They embraced and clinked glasses. They sat down, not at their ease. The bride smiled and said in her sharp voice: "This is good stuff, it slides down smoothly, doesn't it?"

She spoke slowly, searching for words and slightly distorting them.

"You speak good Italian," said Elsa, "you make yourself understood very well."

Mary shook her head and laughed: "I was in Siena a couple of years ago to study music. So I'm fairly familiar with the language." She glanced at Giulio and added: "But I'll improve."

Giulio said at once, his voice turning into a drawl that was almost childlike: "We're hoping to come back to Italy, some day. There are no job opportunities over here for the time being, but even the idea of being stuck there for good. . . ."

The signora poured out some more champagne and

rejoined: "Things do change. And for someone like yourself, it will be easier." She thought of the campus, the clean and spacious streets, the four-square buildings which she had seen in the photographs and went on: "Life out there can't be bad, can it?"

Giulio gestured: so-so. He'd got up and was walking around the room. He stopped to gaze at a hand-coloured print showing the main square of his native town seen from the sea, in pale hues, as in a dream, and between the square and the sea, along the water-front, ran a little pink train. The boy smiled and exclaimed: "But that's Piazza Grande." And, looking at Elsa, he confessed: "On campus, lately, I've been thinking a lot about our town. I wonder why, though. I left when I was twelve, when my father was transferred, d'you remember?"

"I left shortly after, too," said Elsa. She stood up, took a parcel off the shelves and said, handing it to the young man: "So my present for you is well chosen. Here, this is for you two."

Giulio carefully unwrapped the parcel, and made a gesture of surprise: "Where on earth did you find this? Thank you." Mary too was looking at it with curiosity. It was a large embossed-leather album containing old photographs of their town. Giulio started leafing through it slowly. He was saying: "Yes, yes, this is the way I went to school, that's where the momument is and where my grandparents' house used to be." Elsa was looking at them too and the pictures evoked other memories to her mind and she was no longer following Giulio's words. Mary, upon seeing the coast and the light-house, white and slender upon its hilltop, murmured in English: "A lovely little town."

So the three of them remained silent for a while. The young man closed the album and said: "I like this very much, I'll take it back to the States with me."

Elsa broke away and said: "Let's go for dinner. I'll get myself ready, a couple of minutes and I'll be with you."

She went to her bedroom: from there she heard Mary laugh aloud and Giulio ask: "Elsa, we're going out on to the terrace, is that all right?"

There was a warm breath of wind, a door opened noisily, the house had come to life. Elsa's heart, she thought, was beating like a butterfly's wings.

They had dinner in a nearby restaurant. It was still day-light, as the clocks were advanced for summer time, and the waiters in the deserted trattoria were leaning against the door waiting for customers to arrive.

They sat at a secluded table. Mary did not know what to order, and seemed hesitant.

"Fish soup?" suggested the waiter. "It's one of our specialities."

"Have it," insisted Giulio. "Try it, Mary, it's good."

He explained to her in English what it was like, with ten-der looks. Mary nodded agreement, they all ordered the fish soup and the waiter walked off happily.

Elsa looked at the young couple and would have liked to ask them many more questions, but didn't know where to begin and didn't want to be indiscreet, while in the mean-time the waiter returned bringing bread and wine and got Giulio to taste the latter, which he did, saying fine, fine, in some embarrassment.

Elsa sipped at her wine and asked: "What about your studies, Giulio? What exactly are you doing now?"

Giulio grinned and said: "I've been studying the brains of invertebrates for two years." He shook his head, repeating: "I have, I have. Now, on the other hand, I'm studying the anthropoid apes – the gorilla and the chimpanzee." He stop-ped eating and, looking his friend in the face to help her understand more easily, he continued: "It's an almost limit-less subject, we're evolving a behavioural repertoire. You ought to know that the greater apes, like the gorilla, are cap-able of an original response to an object: they sense, for instance, that a stick can be used in a variety of ways, to reach food or to strike a blow." He fell silent, immersed in his own ideas, then continued: "On account of this, I'd say they have an advantage over other species in surviving changes in their environment."

As Giulio spoke, groping for words, Elsa listened, but one part of her, in spite of herself, darted off to encounter distant images: Giulio's mother, standing in front of her, was speaking breathlessly, as she nearly always did: "Oh," she said, "Giulio is bright, he has a scientific mind, like my father, like the men in our family, it's true, you know?" And she shook her thick hair to put more force into her words, then bent her head down, wrung her hands together and kept saying in a low voice: but I'm so uneasy now, I've other things on my mind, other things. Her children were playing in a corner and all about them in the room the atmosphere was grey-blue.

Elsa sighed and, touching the young man on the arm, said: "You must be so clever, a real scientist."

Mary laughed with pleasure and repeated: "Yes, he is very clever. Now I can understand a little, because he explains things so well."

By this time the restaurant was receiving only the waning light of dusk. A waiter walked across and went to turn on the lights.

"So it's over a year since you saw your mother," Elsa reflected mostly to herself, and lost herself gazing into the distance. For a moment she seemed to forget the young couple who fell to talking English together.

The waiter arrived with the dishes and said, addressing his foreign guest: "It's good, you'll see."

Elsa started eating listlessly, because the fish floating in liquid put her off somewhat. Giulio, as he ate, was watching his wife and asked: do you like it? in both languages.

Signora Elsa was also watching the girl who appeared to be suffering from heat and fatigue. She had turned paler and so, sitting down as she was, her dark curly hair gathered up in a little chignon, thin mouth, sharp grey eyes, she looked almost pretty. She smiled at her sympathetically and asked: "And what about your parents, Mary? What do they say? Are they pleased?"

Mary stopped eating and immediately came to life. As she spoke, she made little movements with her neck that apparently helped her in searching for a word. She said: "They're very pleased. They've taken to Giulio. They live in Pennsylvania and we went to see them. But they're not from Pennsylvania, they were born in Chicago. Then they moved in search of a better job. Now my father's in a drugstore and my mother stays at home. My maternal grandmother came from Austria. I never knew her, unfortunately, but Mummy told me lots of stories about her. Giulio says I get my music from her." She ran a hand across her forehead, which was prespiring a little, and murmured:

"Music is very important to me, very important."

Elsa gazed at her, engrossed, her husband also: he stretched his arm out across the table, took her hand, and said in a low voice: "You're lovely, Mary."

A faint blush came over Mary, her eyes sparkled and she laughed aloud.

They set off to catch the bus that was to take the newly-weds back to their hotel. There was still a streak of evening light and the double row of great plane trees were silhouetted against the sky. In the distance loomed the great mass of Porta Pia. It was hot, doorkeepers fanned themselves with newspapers outside open house-doors, the few passers-by idled past in their shirt-sleeves.

Giulio stopped a moment to consult the town map. Signora Elsa took Mary by the arm and said: "Is the conference in Sicily going to be interesting?"

Mary nodded: "Oh, yes," she replied, "it's very important to Giulio that he's been invited to attend."

Elsa went on in a quiet voice: "And after Sicily, you meet his parents."

She smiled to herself as she thought of Giulio's mother, she could see her welcoming the youngsters, arms outstretched, her words overtaking each other. She remarked: "Just think of the excitement."

Mary leaned gently on her arm and replied: "Oh, Giulio tells me so much about them. He speaks so highly of them."

The signora turned to look at the young man with a pang in her heart. For a while she was unable to speak, she made an effort and said: "You needn't worry, Mary. It will all be very easy."

The bus arrived and Giulio ran up to join the two women. They embraced hastily and the couple, holding hands, ran to the bus, Mary climbed in first, somewhat unsteadily and Giulio seemed to be about to prop her up, they turned round together, their two faces close, and cried: "Thank you. Goodbye, goodbye."

Signora Elsa followed them with her eyes, one hand raised in farewell. She started back for home and darkness had fallen.

Shadows

There was somebody in the doorway. There were voices in the corridor and perhaps the front door to the apartment was open. The girl looked up and questioningly eyed the grown-up.

"Go along," said the grown-up. "Go along with the children. Go down into the garden."

The girl took a few steps forward. A taller girl held out her hand and said: "Come on, let's go. Be quick."

They went along the corridor, which was never fully lit, so that you could hardly make out the fine colours of the strip carpet.

They were in the garden and had reached the bottom of the hillock. There were lots of other children shouting and spurring each other on.

"I'm going to climb up. We're going this way, it's the most difficult route."

"Don't you budge, Linda," the bigger girl said to her. "Wait here for me."

"It's a difficult climb for her," she heard the girl tell the others. "It's too difficult. She might fall."

Linda stayed put where she'd been told.

She looked upwards and through the dark foliage of the bushes she was able to make out the beaten tracks that led up to the top of the hillock.

When one of the children reached the summit, he'd shout and stick something into the ground, a twig or a leafy spray. Depending on where they were, Linda would catch sight of legs or an arm and she struggled to imagine what it was like up there, in that forbidden territory, but failed to get any clear idea. Often, terrible scuffles broke out amongst the children that had reached the top, there were shouts and someone or other would break out crying loudly and come down from the hillock with face all red and puffed up with weeping. Then Linda was rather pleased she was incapable of climbing: she remained at her post, bewildered and anxious. But at times she gazed at the steep trails with eager desire, she tried planting her little feet at the beginning of the slope, but shrank back immediately, overcome by fear.

The children came running up, one of them would grab her by the hand and say: "Come on, quick. We're switching our posts."

The whole lot of them were hiding behind tree trunks. Beyond the trees was a clearing, a gravel drive, some earthenware flower-pots and a yellowish house, low but solid.

The children kept still, peeping out carfully, motioning each other to silence. One of them whispered: there she is, she's coming, look – over there. There were chuckles and shufflings of feet.

Linda too was looking upwards. At a middle-floor window, half-way along the house-front, a grey-haired figure had appeared. This person was talking and laughing, raising her arms from time to time. She drew from her bosom a sheet of copy paper, tore it up into tiny pieces and let them fall. They were light and white and looked like petals twirling downwards in the still summer air. The woman leaned over the window-sill to watch their descent. Linda would have liked to emerge from her hiding-place and catch some of the bits, but the bigger girl immediately ordered: don't move, or you'll spoil the fun.

The children in hiding were tittering, but at the same time they had scared looks in their eyes and seemed all set to dash off.

When the woman at the window became aware of their presence, she gave a loud shout, waved her arms about and slammed the shutters to.

Linda, who was watching intently, felt relieved at her disappearance and then immediately regretted the end of that exciting game. During that day, the thought of the woman came back to her with the chatter of the children, of which she had caught a few words: she smokes, son, madwoman.

Linda had entered the deserted sitting-room. A long sunbeam touched the edge of the low table, stamped a rectangle on the floor, picked out the mysterious patterns of the carpets.

The girl had stopped in the middle of the room and was looking round for the picture she enjoyed contemplating: it showed a dark sky – blue, she'd been told – a dark sky broken by a red flare – lightning? – and in the foreground was the black trunk of a tree. When Linda looked at the picture, she felt happy on account of those pretty colours, but also scared because that tree was frightening and behind the trunk, amid the tall grasses, were figures she couldn't make out. She struggled to pick out their outlines, but their shapes eluded her.

The nanny opened the door and said: "What's that child doing here?"

Linda spun round and said: "Nothing."

"You know you're not supposed to come into the sitting-room don't you?"

Linda didn't stir and the nanny continued: "You're being disobedient and now there's a policeman, he's come to fetch you away."

A silence followed. Then a horrible voice cried out, dragging out the syllables and saying: where's that wicked girl? Where is she?

Linda cast down her eyes. She could feel her heart pounding and her eyes tingling. She thought: the policeman is on the other side of that wall, in the dining-room. And she went on thinking: now he'll open the door and fetch me away because I'm wicked. She looked to the nanny for help and thought she was smiling but couldn't grasp why.

Somebody, the policeman, was coming, coughing in his deep tones, she thought she could see him, in fact she was seeing him, she could see his face, his eyes, black and nasty. She bent her head, breathed hard and gazed at the tips of her shoes. The nanny came up to her and said: "What's up, Linda? Come on, don't cry, that was the cook, don't you see? Not a real policeman."

Linda shook her head and breathed out: "No, no, it was the policeman, I'm sure it was."

The nanny bent down and grasped her shoulders. She said, laughing: "Come, come, little one, it was just a little game."

The cook, young and sturdy, came in. She laughed loudly and said: "Silly, it was only me. It was me putting on somebody else's voice. Would you like to hear me?"

Linda said no, no, and shook her head in panic. The two women protested, splitting their sides laughing, they were gap-toothed already. Linda thought confusedly: it's impossible to put on somebody else's voice, to be somebody else. The policeman had been there in the house and had come for her. She glanced quickly round the sitting-room, the sun-beam had worked its way round to the blue painting and the zig-zag streak looked like a gash of blood.

"Well, then," said the cook, "have you stopped sobbing?"

Linda heaved a sigh, the nanny took her by the hand and said imperiously: "There's a good girl, let's go back to your own room."

Linda sat on the white goat-skin rug. She clutched a tuft of shaggy hair in her hands, she liked feeling it even though it was prickly and tickly. Beside her on the rug lay a large open book showing a full-spread black-and-white illustration. The white bits were very bright and contrasted strongly with the black.

The door to her room flew open. A stiff figure stood in the doorway. The door to her room flew open. A stiff figure stood in the doorway. This figure strode across the room, threw open a wardrobe, took a couple of steps towards the child, but as though without seeing her. Linda bent her head and said nothing.

The figure went out, her piercing voice could be heard coming from the corridor saying: my fox-fur. My fox-fur's no longer there. It's gone.

Linda vaguely recalled seeing the female wearing a pearl-grey fur that hid her face, something beautiful to behold. When the person wearing was speaking, the fur quivered. It was most beautiful.

The voice rose again in a rage. It said: there's been a thief in the house, a thief. Something will have to be done.

That heavy stride could be heard going to and fro all round the apartment again, in and out of rooms, snapping wardrobe doors open and shut, the whole apartment seemed overrun by loud and terrible reports.

"Where can she have hidden it?" the voice pursued. "In her parents' house, of course. We must go there, surprise her."

There came the sound of more footsteps, other, less distinct words.

The window framed a sunset-pink sky, but inside the room it was now almost dark and the blacks and whites of the picture-book were disappearing. Linda gazed anxiously at the door to see whether anyone would come to turn on her light.

The nanny took Linda by the arm, without a word she slipped over her a white cotton frock and combed her fair, straight hair.

The girl looked at the frock and smiled: it had smocking with little blue flowers, which she loved. She fingered the flowers and asked: "They're bluebells, aren't they?"

The woman nodded.

"D'you like them?" Linda went on. "D'you like them?"

The woman didn't answer. She slipped on her little cardigan and, looking towards the door, said loudly: "The child's ready."

Linda tried to remove the cardigan because it stopped her from seeing the little blue flowers and besides the wool irritated her bare arms, but the nanny looked at her sternly and ordered: "Keep your cardigan on. You're going out now with your mother and father, you're going for a drive."

Then she heard her father saying: "Are we ready? My friend's waiting downstairs."

He came to the door, picked up the girl and said: "What a pretty dress you're wearing."

Linda smiled, the signora joined them, and without further talk they went down the stairs.

There was silence inside the motor-car. Their friend drove and asked every now and then: "Am I going the right way? Are we sure of the route?"

Her father nodded. They were crossing bleak country, with great rocks everywhere and low trees hunching away from the wind. At one turning the driver slowed down and said: "Look, you can see the sea."

Someone perched Linda on his knees so that she could look out of the window.

"It is lovely," said the signora, "our Adriatic is lovely." And for a moment her face was transformed and her eyes shone with pleasure.

Linda was looking too and saw the expanse of sea far beneath them and repeated: it is lovely, and she was pleased to be saying the same thing as the grown-up, though from that height, almost on the edge of the tall coastal cliffs, the sea seemed different to her from what she was used to seeing every day when she was taken out for walks along the sea-front a few metres from the water, and she could smell its strong tang.

The car resumed its journey and turned inland, they reached a small village and the man's voice said: "This is it. Let's get out. The house is just on the edge of the village."

They crossed an open space and turned up a path. The air was full of fragrances and the gentleman filled his lungs and said: what clean air they have up here. A herd of cows was coming towards them, blocking the lane and swishing their tails against their flanks. The child came to a standstill, her father took her hand and said: "They're gentle. And with their great eyes you look big to them. So they're scared of you."

This idea engaged her for a good while. She couldn't grasp it and at the same time she imagined herself as bigger than a grown-up and that made her smile.

She stood in an open space not too far away from the house which her parents had entered. The gentleman who had driven the car was with her. He had lit himself a cigarette in gilt paper, looked smilingly at her and said:

"One of these mornings I shall come bathing. I really want to see whether you're scared of the water."

Linda made no reply. She gazed at the house with the pitched roof and the wide-open door. Excited voices could be heard: a man was shouting louder and louder; a girl came out of the house crying, she ran hunched forward and crying: I don't know a thing, I don't know a thing, and as she ran her hair had come undone and fallen about her shoulders, behind her came the old peasant-farmer waving a strap, pursuing her and trying to hit her with it and now and then the black strap could be seen in the bright air and a crack would be heard.

The gentleman muttered something and took Linda by the hand. He dragged her off towards the edge of the field where the fruit trees were, Linda followed him obediently but it was as if she had eyes in the back of her head and she could see that girl all red and sobbing and the man swinging his strap up in the air.

In the car, the signora was clasping in her hands the fox-fur that was so light and beautiful and trembled at every movement. They were going fast and stones could be heard pattering against the mudguards. Along the sides of the unsurfaced road the occasional bare-foot child raised a hand in greeting. The sky had darkened and the upland rock looked whiter still against that backdrop. The grown-ups looked straight ahead of them, tight-lipped and vacant-eyed. After they rounded a bend, something glittered in the distance. Linda raised herself a little and pointing her finger towards the grey-blue expanse that suddenly opened out in front of them, lilted: there's the sea. She looked anxiously at the grown-ups, but none of them spoke. The child felt something heavy come all over her and didn't know how to shake it off.

Someone – the nanny? – had turned the light off. A knife-edge of light came into the room from the corridor, a few objects reflected a faint gleam, she could make out the netting that enclosed one side of her bed.

There was the sound of footsteps in the passage, agitated but subdued voices. Then nothing more. The door to her room opened and Linda heard or felt a grown-up breathing close by, but she kept her eyes closed and did not move.

Each thinking her own thoughts

We were sitting face to face, my aunt Miriam and I, in the great room which was full of light as the hospital's glass front looked south. And on one side, past the garden, could be seen the dunes of the Alberoni and the glittering sea, and, on the other side, the lagoon's horizontal and magical lines. We'd had a long talk about her illness, her convalescence and her difficulty in getting settled somewhere. Then my aunt said: "Last year I was still in pretty good shape. So I went to Istria with my cousin Lorenza to visit our dead in the graveyard. And I also paid a visit to my old house. You used to come and stay there as a child, do you remember it?"

She went on: "I went through the front door, Lorenza was with me. A partition divided it in two, so that I scarcely recognized it. A woman went past and Lorenza entreated her: this lady is the former owner of this house and she'd like to have a look round. The woman made great sweeping gestures to say yes, we could go upstairs and downstairs, wherever we pleased."

My aunt paused. She began stroking her hands, raised them up for my examination and remarked: "D'you see? Swollen veins, sclerosis. It's a bad sign, something's wrong."

"Tell me more," I insisted. "Tell me what your house looks like now."

As a child, whenever I went through that great entrance, chilly and shadowy, I was more scared and timorous than usual and I'd hope my uncle wasn't in, but didn't have the courage to ask whether he was. In any case, some clue or other would soon give away his presence, the dog barking, the horse-whip hanging from its hook or his bawling that could be heard from the road and made my aunt turn red and mutter to herself: why does he yell so, why does he have to yell?

I would spend Saturday and Sunday at my uncle and aunt's. I'd wait for my father to come and see me there: so the time went by in expectation of his visit, in a state of vague apprehension.

I felt ill at ease in a house that was so different from the ones I knew, I didn't know what to do with myself in those huge interiors which had no obvious use, superfluous, as my aunt called them. Particularly when I'd just arrived, I'd move slowly, my knees felt stiff, I'd keep my eyes downcast and speak in a low voice, and if my uncle was at home he'd yell: well, has your niece lost her voice? Hasn't she got a tongue? I'd linger with relief in a secluded and ill-lit area, at the foot of the stairs, or I'd settle myself in front of the hearth and gaze and gaze at the skilled movements of my aunt or the maid as they raised and replaced the iron hoops. Behind the hearth was a broad window which opened on to the terrace, so that from where I was, snug and warm, I could see the sky, the geraniums and my aunt's cats.

Aunt Miriam leaned back in her armchair with a vivacious move and a twinkle in her eye and I thought she was going to laugh.

"There's nothing left," she said. "Walls and partitions and extra floors have been put in everywhere. Even the kitchen is unrecognizable. The hearth's gone, the great window's been partly bricked up, that fine old seventeenth-century archway at the foot of the stairs has been taken down. Lorenza was pale, she looked around and kept saying: I can't stand it, I feel ill, they've made such a mess of it. But I didn't mind a bit." She looked me in the eye as if to convince me that she meant it and repeated: "It didn't bother me at all to see my house look like that."

I looked down and let slip: but what a shame. I could see myself crossing the kitchen and the great hall, it was full of people, they were celebrating the engagement of a nephew of my uncle's and the bride's relatives had come from afar. The sunshine streaming in through the French windows brightened up the ruby-coloured quarry-tiles of the floor. People were talking loudly, my aunt moved round slowly in her new dress that was close-fitting around her broad hips, my uncle was talking about his little town and looked the peaceful country gentleman.

The sun was close to setting and the white of the walls and

the bedsheets in the ward was greying. My aunt was touching her hands and looking at her veins and shaking her head. I avoided her gaze, but couldn't help asking her: "Why did you marry uncle?"

"I've asked myself the same thing so many, many times," she answered slowly. "It was just after the end of the war in 1918. He used to come and see my cousins. One day he came at an unusual time and spoke to my poor uncle, who was also my guardian, and asked for my hand. I was most astonished, I really wasn't expecting it, but I must have thought it was my destiny. Round about that time my guardian had been widowed and had fallen in love with a lady. I still remember him always in a rush to go out and I and my cousins from the window would watch him run to catch the tram. Perhaps I thought he was dying to get me off his hands."

I followed what she said attentively, and as my aunt was being so confiding, I enquired: "But didn't you feel anything for him? Didn't you even like him a little bit?"

She pursed her lips and said: "No, I never liked him. Not even the first time we met." She shifted slowly on her seat and said: "Would you fetch me a handkerchief. Look inside the wardrobe, first on the right."

I got up and opened the small white wardrobe: there were biscuit tins which her visitors had brought her, some laundry which had been put away hastily, and her dressing-gown. I murmured: what a collection of confectionery.

"Yes," said my aunt, "but I don't feel like eating any of it."

I went back to her and handed her the handkerchief. She wiped her forehead, which was perspiring slightly, looked away and asked: "But do you remember him? Do you remember how he shouted?"

I couldn't help smiling, and nodded. Uncle would peel a peach, slice it up, and put the slice in his glass. His tenant farmer would come in with a basketful of grapes, little golden bunches. The maid would shuffle around muttering to herself from time to time. Uncle would yell out irate commands to the farmer and then cry: I'm off; he'd go out and we'd hear the roar of his motor-cycle deafening the little alley. My aunt would pick up her favourite cat and say: d'you see how lovely he is? The cat would purr and I would stroke him too and I'd say to my aunt: may I comb your hair? Let's go to the other room and I'll comb you. And I'd feel her raven-black hair which was as thick as a skein of wool.

A nun in a white habit appeared, tinkled her keys, smiled and gave the greeting: "Our Lord be praised."

"Be he praised for ever," murmured my aunt.

"How are we doing? All right?" asked the nun, already on the point of leaving.

"As usual," replied my aunt. "The same as ever."

We remained silent. The nun had gone and we could hear her voice and the jingling of her keys recede further and further down the ward. My aunt was reclining back against her seat again and pursuing who knows what train of thought. She pursed her lips as she so often did and said: "Do you know, I tried to get away from him once. It was during the years when he kept chasing women and spending money on them. So I ran away from home and went to stay with my sister in the countryside. On his way to my sister's to bring me back home, he had a motor-cycle accident and broke a femur. So in the end I went back to nurse him." She hesitated an instant and added: "At times I've felt that the whole story of the accident was an invention of his."

"What?" I exclaimed. "Is it possible?"

She nodded. "He was even capable of that."

She had grown mournful as she spoke and her pupils trembled for an instant. I thought of my uncle: the last time I saw him was in winter, in war-time. Their house, after such a long interval, felt smaller to me. His dog had died, the country people had poisoned it out of hatred for its master. I'd found my uncle sitting in his armchair beside the cast-iron stove. On seeing me, his grey eyes flickered with curiosity, but he barely greeted me. His face, even through the pallor of his illness, was still handsome.

I murmured: "He died during the war, didn't he?"

"Yes," replied my aunt. "And that was just as well, considering what happened afterwards. She pressed her wine-red dressing-gown to her chest and continued "I tended him during the day and went back home every evening. I remember, on that morning they sent for me very early, I rushed over, but when I arrived he was already dead. After the funeral, I busied myself with reorganizing the house. I'd hardly ever entered his study, he wouldn't allow it. I found his collection of knives, I knew he collected them, but I had no idea he had so many. They were set out in an old cupboard, all sorts and sizes: bill-hooks, pen-knives, cleavers."

As she spoke, her eyes seemed to drift off, the hollows round them grew deeper. She ended: "I threw them all away, they frightened me."

Someone had turned the television on in the common room and we could hear the announcer's loud voice. Then chairs were grated on the floor and there was some bustle in the corridor.

"Shall I shut the door?" I asked. I got up, pushed the door to, and went up to the window. I attempted to contemplate the open sea, but my eyes were looking at another seascape, bluer and wind-swept. Aunt Miriam was beside me, saying: The wind's from the south-west, it's lovely when it blows from the south-west. She'd give me her hand, we'd walk up and down the quay and she'd talk to me as to a big girl. Across the creek, the shoreline sparkled, white rocks in the sun. Sometimes we'd wait on that quay for my father to arrive by the morning boat. He'd hurry down the gangway with head thrust forward and shoulders hunched. On the way home, they talked away so fast that I couldn't follow, so I'd count the paving slabs along our route and invented games for myself.

I returned to my aunt, smiled and said vivaciously: "Well, you don't look bad, quite the opposite."

"No, no," she replied. "There's a new problem bothering me now, the problem of the cat."

I looked at her uncomprehendingly.

"Yes," she explained. "My next-door neighbour tells me that my cat has gone wild, and she's afraid of opening the door to feed it. She says it might be sick. I wonder if there's any truth in that. But I've no choice in the matter and I've asked her to do the necessary but not to tell me about it. I don't want to know."

She brought her head close to mine, lowered her voice and began speaking slowly. She said: "It's a strange animal, you know. It's always been dotty, it wasn't like other cats. It was only attached to me. Whenever anyone else appeared, it would hide under the bed. That's why nobody cares for it."

Her eyes wandered this way and that and turned hard, like

small dark stones. I kept still, I could think of nothing to say and I was trying to catch – or to dismiss? – a voice in the sunshine from long, long ago, saying: but I know your aunt Miriam very well, she was lovely, it's painful to see her stuck with a man like that.

The lagoon was fading into darkness and dimming the great windows until they showed black.

A nun came in and said: "In the dark, ladies?" — and lit the main light. She added: "It will be dinner-time soon."

I waited for the nun to leave and asked in a low voice: "Is the food good here?"

"So-so," replied my aunt, "They could do better."

The orderly wheeled in a heavy trolley, bread, wine and cutlery and said: "It's soup with pasta today."

"And yesterday?" returned my aunt imperturbably.

"Ah, ha," said the orderly more loudly, "pasta soup is good for you in the evening. Very good for you."

We were left alone again. I set the bread and wine on the little table-cloth and asked: "Will you have some wine?"

"Yes," said my aunt, "a drop of wine does no harm."

I handed her the glass with a smile. The moment had come for us to say goodbye and we embraced warmly.

Shortly after, I was on the trolley-bus retracing the route that would take me to the landing-stage and from there to the railway station. I could not stop thinking of my aunt. But suddenly, in the dark, on the lagoon side, there appeared a great vessel festively illuminated and it was beautiful and spectral.

Concentric group

The old lady slightly raised her head, took up the binoculars and, training them on a distant point, said: The horses. There they are.

Along the beach, silhouetted against the clear sky, two riders were moving at a beautiful canter. The old lady lowered her binoculars and smiled. Her smile slowly faded, she appeared paler, raised her eyelids ever so slightly and began in a neutral voice:

I'm sorry to see Angelo in this state. Up to some time ago he was different, he even used to come and see me here and talk. He used to say: Auntie, listen. And I was happy to listen to him and glad I had his confidence, though he was little more than a boy. He's changed now, he comes to see me rarely, says: I've brought you this, is there anything you need? And he rushes off again.

He's a fine, tall, strong lad. But he isn't as fit as he appears. He often feels poorly, he gets headaches, and you can tell right away by his colour and his eyes that he's not well. The business with that girl is over now. To my mind, she was a bright girl and well suited to him in that respect, but they've parted. I don't know which of them left the other, Angelo didn't talk much about her, he often said: We did so-and-so, we saw so-and-so, but didn't name her. He told me a lot about her just once. That day he was in good spirits, I remember he'd just been fencing and was still in his white uniform, which became him very well and showed up his dark curly hair. He demonstrated a few positions and I asked: Do you still enjoy fencing? 'Yes,' he said, 'I like it because it's so ceremonial, it's a kind of acting.' He told me his girl-friend didn't get on with his mother, the two women couldn't stand each other, which was a real problem. And he added: She's a good friend to me, we're okay, we'll have to see. I don't mind having an open relationship –

very open. I was struck by this, didn't know what to make of it, but I didn't have the courage to ask him exactly what he meant. So the conversation moved on.

That was when he was a student and involved in other things as well, like so many young men. Of course, he's always had plenty of interests. He's teaching now, and sometimes he's happy and relates little incidents, but usually he's surly. However, if you talk about the future, about other possibilities, he withdraws into his shell and brings up all sorts of reasons against making a change.

When I think of Angelo and his young days, my mind wanders off to our own youth and I always end up reminiscing about my brother Alvise. Towards the end of his life my brother disliked travelling, so his nephew Angelo never came to know him as well as I'd have wished. Regarding Alvise, I had an experience which I still can't explain and which goes on troubling me. It was just seven years ago, I was going along the little avenue from the church to my house, the sun was setting and it began to get dark straight away because it was the end of August and you know what that part of town is like, the houses are low, the trees have grown large and the sea gives a dull, dank atmosphere. So, dusk was falling, and, as I was returning home, raising my eyes, twice over I had the impression that I could see Alvise walking towards me with his diffident gait and his half-smile, and the second time the impression was so strong that I called out: Alvise, Alvise, is that you? I was a bit distraught when I reached home and immediately told Angelo's mother: I thought I'd just seen Alvise, you know, Maria? I really thought I was looking at him. And Angelo's mother answered: You know that can't be so, Alvise's away on a journey.

The next day there was a phone-call from somewhere in the South. It was the police, reporting that Alvise had been involved in a motorway accident and had died on the way to hospital.

When we were young we all thought life would come easy to Alvise. He was so gifted and popular, he shone at school but took his successes lightly and everybody liked him. He was studying medicine when the world war broke out and he was immediately drafted into the medical corps. I've kept a postcard photograph of him, which he sent me from the front. It shows him in his white overall with two Sisters of Canossa, one on either side of him and a group of convalescent soldiers, and in the background you could make out the iron bedsteads, the tricolor rosette and a crucifix. My brother's face looks gentle and drawn. On the card he wrote: My dear sister, don't I really look a great doctor? As soon as I have time, I'll send you a long letter.

But he didn't write much and even after the war was reluctant to talk about his experiences. I recall my mother at first used to question him, kept asking him: Why don't you tell me about all those months out there? Alvise would look at her, wave his hand as if it were all so far away, and reply: Some other time.

Towards the end of the war he was wounded in the foot and spent a long time in hospital because the wound, which had seemed a slight one, wouldn't heal. Perhaps the war and being an invalid brought about a greater change in him than we realized at the time, or maybe not – maybe that's just the way he was. Our parents were already elderly and were upset because Alvis wasn't getting on with his medical studies and I remember especially how it grieved my mother that the son she doted on hadn't yet settled down. So an uncle, Alvise's godfather, decided to make the journey to see for himself what was actually going on. It was I who saw him off when he caught the coach. It had been blowing a gale for days and the ferries weren't sailing. So my uncle had to take the coach as far as the main town and then continue the journey by train. At that time we were living in a sunny position just outside the town gate on an unsurfaced country road. When my uncle returned, we were thrown into utter dismay: he had found out that the pain from his wound had made Alvise addicted to morphine.

That was about the time I got married and left our little town. I did see Alvise from time to time, but it was always on family occasions and it was difficult to talk heart-to-heart. And what could we have said? We understood each other: at our leave-takings he would embrace me warmly and whisper: 'I'm always thinking of you, you know?' And once he said: 'I'm always here when you want me, remember that.' But I didn't want to upset him.

He and I were the youngest in the family and close to each

other in age, so we'd done lots of things together and had many memories in common. When we were children we often used to spend the day in the country at our maternal uncle and aunt's: we had to get there either by pony-trap or on a small boat. It was a lovely spot, with pine trees coming right down to the sea, vineyards higher up, fruit orchards and maize fields. I remember the golden glow, the patches of sunlight in among the trees, the sound of the sea on the rocky shore and us children scampering about in that Eden of ours, and I think – it makes my heart beat to say this – I think: 'That is where I was full of joy, that is where I felt more light-hearted than I've ever been since.'

I'd occasionally chat away to Angelo and also to his sister Livia about our bit of land there by the sea, which they don't know because it's been on the other side of the border since the war and hardly any of us have ever felt like going back. We used to talk about it non-stop with their mother, our uncles and aunts, with our friends from those bygone times who would sometimes turn up suddenly from somewhere or other, and Angelo and Livia often used to laugh at our interminable chatter and exclaim: 'Here, my dears, we're still living before the war, here we're still stuck in '38.' But in the end Angelo and Livia themselves began asking about the things and mentioning the names that were so familiar to us as if they'd been there too or else they'd say: You are lucky, it must have been lovely to spend your childhood there. It must have been very different. Once Angelo even dreamed he was at our place in the country and related the dream to me afterwards. He dreamed he was in the clearing in front of the farmhouse among the oleanders in their great pots clutching a baby rabbit, but he clutched it so hard that the rabbit died in his hands. The incident really did happen to me when I was a little girl: my uncle and aunt had given me a little white rabbit and I was so thrilled that I would run over to look at it whenever I could, I'd feed it and hold it in my arms. One day I inadvertently squeezed it too hard and found I was holding a dead creature. It was awful, I couldn't understand it, I cried, I was in despair, and nobody could calm me down. And during the night, as they told me later, I woke up with a start several times, shrieking. I think the idea of death coming so suddenly must have shaken me. It must all have been very vague in my mind because I was tiny – I couldn't have been more than seven – and I kept asking myself: How could I – I who loved it – do it harm?

Alvise perhaps might have been able to explain it to me. He understood people. After many uncertainties, he had qualified as a doctor, the patients in the small town where he went to practise spoke highly of him. After he died I met an old friend of his who is a famous doctor. He had asked to see me and we spent a long while going over the past. Before he left, he said: I can't set my mind at rest. Alvise was the best among us, but he always refused to put himself forward and he could never do the tiniest thing that was contrary to his nature. And what did he get out of it?

Were my brother here now, I would put it to him: Why did you lead the life you led? He probably wouldn't answer. He'd give me a quizzical look, as was his wont, a deep, deep look, and I'd understand and ask no more questions. Alvise generally didn't like talking about himself. In the course of his life there were some periods when he sank into deep depression: he'd withdraw into long silences and it would seem as though everything, absolutely everything, had palled on him.

But I was talking to you about Angelo. He was different as a student. He was more self-assured, sometimes he even seemed elated. He had a girl-friend and they were both part of a group of young people. He'd come and go, vanish for days on end and one of his friends would let his mother know that Angelo would be coming back soon. This happened quite often, and naturally caused some anxiety, but isn't there always a bit of anxiety in thinking about young people? We really don't know much about that time of his life, I didn't ask his mother any questions, and she didn't confide in me. On just one occasion his sister Livia spoke to me about him and let me into a secret that was weighing on her mind. One night Angelo had turned up at their house, apparently agitated, and had asked her and her husband if he could stay a while. All those days he remained agitated, a friend used to come and see him in the evening and they would shut themselves up in his room to talk. In the end Angelo told Livia: I've got to take a decision, but I feel I can't go through with it, I just can't. As he said those words he had gone very pale and he stood leaning against the door-post staring, a pitiful sight. Livia tried to find out more, but Angelo kept repeating: I'll tell you some day. But he never said a thing about what had happened. When Livia told me about the incident, her brother had graduated, had changed his circle of friends and was looking for a job.

He started coming to see me again. I was pleased when he came, I was still in my own home and Angelo would turn up unannounced, sit down at his ease and we'd have a chat. He often asked me about the past, about the family, and with him I'd relive forgotten experiences. We argued occasionaly because I ticked him off for being inconsistent: You waste time, you lose interest in things too easily, like your fencing, which you were so good at. Angelo would smile and protest: You're wrong, I'm not wasting time, it's all experience.

Now he's taken up singing. He says he's always wanted to and blames his mother for not having let him learn music from childhood. He's hired a piano and found a young instructor. His mother says he's applying himself to it passionately. She tells me that Angelo and his piano-teacher have become very friendly and go to the opera and to concerts together. When I hear this music-teacher being mentioned, I think of the wicked world we live in and feel very sad.

Very often Angelo and I would sit facing each other without saying anything, and if the sun was setting we'd go out on to the balcony from where we could see the sea, and we'd stand there looking at it. Angelo likes the sea, too: early in the morning, if he's able, he goes for long walks along the beach and tells me that the tide brings in the strangest objects, and sometimes he collects them. Where *we* lived it was different because the coast was rocky. It's an attractive coast, bright and varied, the rocks aren't very high.

When I left my house for good, I gave Angelo a picture which had been Alvise's. It shows the sunset seen from our

164

land with low rocks emerging from the calm sea like sheep and the sheet of water appears iridescent, being fairly shallow. A long way off on the coast you can see the nearest houses of the village: as they face north, they're in shadow. I was very fond of that picture. I would often gaze at it and as I did so I'd recall so much of our youth, but in the end I no longer thought of anything: I was there in that light, bright over the horizon, but already fainter along the deserted shore.

Yesterday evening Angelo's sister came to see me here at the home. She isn't the slender thing she once was. Now she's a large woman, not very well-groomed. I think it's the contraceptives that have made her like that. They don't want to have children. Her husband's brother has been a problem ever since he was born and has caused his family so much heartache. Perhaps Livia's husband is right not to want to have anything to do with children. I heard all this from Livia's mother – *she* never talks about it, she's got a shy and reticent nature.

When I look at Livia, I see myself. You go on and on this way through the years and solitude casts a longer and longer shadow: the gap between you and the next person grows hopelessly wide, nothing can span it.

Sometimes I dream I'm at the window of my house, I can see the house opposite and there on the balcony are arrayed all my family, the old people in front and the young ones behind. There's no one on the street. And I call out to them, I keep calling louder and louder, but nobody hears me, nobody stirs. I know there's something in the air that dissolves sound.

Assignments in Africa

Per Wästberg

This is a very personal book, written by a man with an intimate knowledge of the people and politics of Africa. It is at once exciting, poetic and thought-provoking. As Wästberg travels, the conflicts and problems of Africa become easier to understand. He tells us of meetings with people and with nature in East Africa, Zambia, Botswana, Swaziland and Mozambique.

At the heart of his journey lies a concern with the struggle against racism in southern Africa, symbolised by the time he spent at the home of Eduardo Mondlane, founder of Frelimo. The author has been in contact with the various southern African liberation movements over many years and demonstrates, sadly, how little has changed.

"Per Wästberg has the deep insights of a fine novelist and playwright combined with the clear analytical intelligence of a superb journalist. The result is reportage of southern Africa in a new and striking perspective, gathered from wide experience and reflection. He takes at once the long and the intimate view, with the terrible conflict in South Africa placed in the context of the power it radiates in political and human consequences through sub-Saharan Africa. His publisher is to be congratulated on making this important selection of his work available to English-speaking readers." Nadine Gordimer

"Through his grasp of a complex situation and his compassionate concern for individuals, Per Wästberg has written a book which should be required reading for understanding this turbulent continent." André Brink

£5.95 $8.95 pbk ISBN 0 946889 11 2 pbk
£10.95 $15.95 hbk ISBN 0 946889 12 0 hbk

The Scent of India

Pier Paolo Pasolini

"Moment by moment, there is a smell, a colour, a sense which is India". So wrote Pasolini in this collection of essays describing his visit to India with fellow authors Alberto Moravia and Elsa Morante. This book captures the shimmering, magical quality of India, while at the same time Pasolini's critical eye records the terrible poverty that accompanies it.

Though widely admired as a film director, Pasolini's talents as a poet, essayist and social critic are not generally known outside Italy. His ability to portray the dreamlike yet earthy quality of a country, which showed so clearly in his films, comes through in this book.

"Pasolini's journey . . . is chronicled with characteristically feeling perceptiveness." *Times Literary Supplement*

£4.95 $7.95 pbk ISBN 0 946889 02 3

Alphabet City

David Price

As his marriage disintegrates in a welter of suspicion and accusation, Peter begins to discover a homosexual identity of which he was previously unaware. He tries to escape his past and recreate his identity by fleeing to America. There he is drawn into the bleak sub-culture of lower Manhattan and at the same time into a devouring relationship with Joe, a black actor. The two of them leave on a dare-devil trip, running drugs through the South-Western States, a trip which takes on the mysterious contours of pursuit and self-destruction . . .

"David Price has extracted the heart of New York and delivered it alive and throbbing on the page. This is the underworld that few tourists ever see . . . David Price has seen it with great clarity." *Edmund White*

"The novel's core of a man launching out in search of transcendent passion is winningly and sharply presented." *Time Out, London*

"The sentences harmonize like the themes of a fugue. And the resulting structure, durable and inviting, satisfies like a contemporary tonal symphony." Stan Leventhal, *Torso*

£3.50 $6.50 pbk ISBN 0 946889 00 7
£7.95 $14.50 hbk ISBN 0 946889 08 2

A Little Murder

Marie Stone

"The Anselmo baby is dead. Its body was found this evening in a public toilet in Great Marlborough Street." Katie
closed her eyes, red-grey sparkling shapes whirled about.
When she turned, through eyes full of tears, she saw the
blurred shapes of the detectives standing in the kitchen
doorway.

The unruly family upstairs scarcely affect Katie Brown's
independent lifestyle working in an expensive clothes store
in the West End of London, until she finds herself implicated
in theft, kidnap and murder.

A Little Murder is an accurately observed and finely
detailed study of one woman's life in a big city.

"Marie Stone's updating of the conventions of lifestyle,
character and setting of a Barbara Pym-style novel." *City
Limits*

£4.50 $7.95 pbk ISBN 0 946889 05 8
£7.95 $14.50 hbk ISBN 0 946889 06 6